Spooky Basement 1:
Welcome to Monsteropolis

Clay Astroman

For Cool Idiots
www.spookybasement.com
www.forcoolidiots.com

Fourth edition printed 2019.

Art by Neil Astroman: www.iceandshadows.blogspot.com
For Cool Idiots
Printed by CreateSpace
ISBN: 9781547146024

spookybasement@gmail.com

"I love deadlines. I love the whooshing noise they make as they go by." –Douglas Adams

Dedicated to all of the Indiegogo backers, especially the one of you I don't personally know. You're a solid dude, Mark.

1

Baron crashed into his throne, tore open an envelope, and began reading intensely. His guitar and best friend, Garindax, hung above him from a massive spike on the wall.

Garindax was blacker than the blackest witch butthole and older than the oldest witch butthole. He had a body shaped like a spider's head, with neon purple tone knobs for eyes and inverse jacks that also served as poisonous fangs. His neck was a twisted mass of nails, and his frets glowed in the dark or light—it didn't even matter.

Oh, yeah, he could also talk.

"Yo, Baron, what's that you're reading?" he asked his best friend in the universe.

"It's an invitation to Little Billy's birthday party," Baron replied to his best friend in the universe.

"Baller ass! I love LB. When and where?"

"Right now, at PizzArea 64."

"Don't you mean PizzArea 51?"

"No. That place exploded, remember? You were there. We both were."

"Yeah, of course. It was, uh, legit."

Garindax *didn't* remember, and he was intentionally vague so it would sound like he thought PizzArea 51 was legit in case Baron had dug it, or the explosion that destroyed it in case he hadn't. Garindax was far more insecure than any blacker-than-butthole spider guitar monster should be.

He flew off the wall and landed on the ground next to Baron, digging his fangs into the carpet and injecting some venom into it for good measure.

"Alright, man, let's go hit this up," Baron said as he rose from his throne made of shark bones and dental floss.

Garindax vommed out a frothy web guitar strap, and Baron slung his buddy over his shoulder. Normally, the strap's crazy acidity would've melted right through someone who did that, slicing him in half like a mushy banana.

But not Baron.

Baron was too tough, and too pumped.

He slammed his boots together to activate their jet thrusters, and the duo took off into the sky toward PizzArea 64.

"We're here, dude. Wake up," Baron said after a super long flight.

Garindax had gone into hibernation mode during the trip in order to conserve his power for the party. While he slept, he dreamt of orangutan ghosts who screamed as they watched a group of chimps play bongos on their skulls (not their own skulls, but the orangutans' skulls).

Now he was awake and staring up at PizzArea 64. It looked amazing: like PizzArea 51, but with an expansion pack.

The entire building was shaped like a flying saucer, and it was painted with mercury so it shined like crazy and made you feel sick if you stood too close to it.

A neon "PizzArea 64" sign pulsed violently and changed colors from orange to black to red to green, so whether it was Halloween or Christmas, you got pumped/primed.

"Fart yeah. Let's tear this party apart," Baron whispered because Garindax was slowly waking up, and he wanted to be respectful of that.

As the duo busted up to the threshold, the front door swung open even though they hadn't grabbed the handle or stepped on one of those magic mats or *anything*.

Slowly, but also really confidently, Baron and Garindax walked into PizzArea 64. As soon as they entered, a voice asked, "Are you boys here to die tonight?"

2

Baron searched for the location of the voice, which sounded like it came from a French baby standing at the bottom of a mountain.

It actually came from the maître d', who stood at PizzArea 64's PedCheck gate. A PedCheck gate is where someone, usually/ironically a ped, stamps your hand with a unique identifier to make sure a stranger doesn't try to leave with you. The only rad thing about PedCheck gates is that the stamps tend to be UV-sensitive, so there's usually a blacklight chilling somewhere nearby. This can provide a solid mini pump upon entering, and potentially a max pump upon exiting as long as you were smart enough to turn your tickets into glow-in-the-dark spiders or something.

"What the fuck did you just say to us, you little bitch?" Baron demanded.

"Excusez-moi, sir," the maître d' replied pompously with his neck fat jiggling all over the place. His face was melty and gross, and his eyes were almost shut from his dumb grin and even dumber fat.

"I merely said, 'are you boys here to *dine* tonight?'"

"Oh, I must've misheard you," Baron replied with a manic smile. "You should really learn to speak up."

He pulled out a razor guitar pick and threw it into the maître d's throat.

The probably-a-ped screamed, and the French modulations made the guitar pick cut wider and deeper until his neck split down the middle and his head flipped backward.

Blood spewed everywhere, and the maître d's tongue stood straight up in the air and danced around like an idiot. He fell to the ground, either dead or really close to it.

Baron grabbed the PedCheck stamp off the counter and stamped his hand/Garindax's fretboard.

"Can't be too safe," he chuckled.

He threw the stamp onto the maître d's stomach with such force that it rocketed his tongue out of his neck-hole and almost into a skeeball machine's "50" slot, but of-fucking-course it bounced out and impotently rolled into the 10, which might as well have been 0.

Baron and Garindax busted into the main area of PizzArea 64 and up to the food counter. A teenager, glowing orange from spray tan and wearing an upside-down visor, greeted them.

"*Hey-ee-aay!*" she rasped with a Valley Gutter accent. "Y'all here for the *part-aaay?*"

"Maybe," Baron replied coolly. "But even if we were, we never party on an empty stomach. Give us two pizzas, large. X-Treme sour watermelon for me, hot blue razz for my friend here."

"Your friend?" the girl replied, licking her lips and leaning in toward Baron's crotch. "I'd love to meet him."

"Your wish is my command, babe."

Baron swung Garindax off his shoulder, slamming the teen in the head and sending cobalt blue sparks flying into the sky.

The girl fell back against the wall and gurgled like a confused sheep.

"Now, about that 'za," Baron demanded.

With her last ounce of strength, the teen reached up from the ground and dinged a little bell. Behind her, metal kitchen doors exploded open and fog poured into the room.

A crazed chef, obese but that kind of obese where he still has a four-pack and giant muscles busting through his chef clothes, slowly walked out of the kitchen.

He held a massive meat cleaver in each ham-hock hand, drool dripped from his mustachioed lip, and his eyes glazed and twitched in pure intensity.

He was the absolute embodiment of pissed/pumped.

"*SOOO*, you want some 'za, do ya?!" he screamed, spitting saliva and bits of ravioli onto the now-dead teenage worker.

"Come and fuck' get it!"

3

The obese chef charged at Baron and swung his right meat cleaver.

Baron jumped back, but the cleaver grazed him and sliced off a few eyebrows. As he watched them flutter to the floor, he realized that this dude wasn't messing around.

So without further hesitation, Baron grabbed Garindax and started shredding.

He alternated between power chords and high notes so seamlessly that it sounded like four people were playing at once: one focusing on power chords and the other three on notes, but maybe sometimes two and two.

The chef instantly became so mesmerized that a trickle of pee ran down his leg. He hoped no one noticed, but everyone did and talked about it later. One kid even drew a picture of it from memory that night, and when his mom found it she put the kid in therapy without telling him or his dad the reason because she thought that was her way of "protecting them," but when she finally mentioned it one night when the kid was in his 20's and she was drunk on chardonnay, shit really hit the fan.

As Baron held a final note on the 75th fret, bending it in an infini-wail, a black hole appeared in front of him. Chameleon-paint skeleton arms shot out of the void and grabbed the chef's face really hard.

"Time out, time out!" the chef cried, swinging his arms wildly in circles.

"No way, José," Baron replied, repulsed by his foe's display of wimpiness.

Garindax nervously scanned the room in case anyone thought Baron was being racist because the chef sort of looked Hispanic, but everyone was cool about it.

The skeleton hands squeezed the chef's cheeks (face, not butt) even harder while he continued to flail around like a drunk chicken.

After an hour and with a wet *POP!* the chef's head snapped off and soared across PizzArea 64, spritzing blood everywhere before dropping straight through the hoop of a basketball redemption game. Tickets exploded out of the machine and sirens went nuts, announcing the highest score in history.

"And one, baby," Baron muttered as he stepped over the chef's corpse and into the kitchen.

After chowing down hard on pizza, Baron and Garindax were finally ready to join Little Billy's birthday party.

But that's when Baron realized something that stopped him dead in his tracks/pump:

They had totally forgotten to bring a present.

"Dude, what are we going to do?" Baron asked in a panic. "We don't have shit to give LB!"

"Yo, waitwaitwait," Garindax said reassuringly. "Isn't it, um, soft-shell crab season?"

"What the fuck?" Baron snapped. "Who would know that? Why do *you* know that?"

"I *don't* know. That's why I was asking."

"Well, I sure as fuck don't know either."

"Oh."

There was an uncomfortable silence, where the only sound came from an arcade machine shouting "Bingo!" over and over again.

"Dude," Baron started again as calmly as possible. "Why did you bring up crabs when we should be freaking out over Little Billy's gift?"

"Well, that's just it. I was thinking we could give him some—one, if they're expensive—as his birthday present."

"This is fucking *LB* we're talking about," Baron said as pissed as possible. "The same LB, who for *your* birthday, gave you a guitar pedal that turns all your notes into fart noises—batteries included. And you want to give him *crabs?*"

"*Soft-shell* crabs."

"What the fuck even is that? A pet?"

"I don't know. I just keep hearing people talking about them. That's why I was hoping you'd be down. So we could find out together."

Baron palm-muted Garindax. He needed to think.

As his eyes followed the trail of blood left by the chef's head, he noticed the snake of tickets still crawling out of the basketball machine. There had to be at least a thousand there already.

"Garindax," he said, unmuting his annoying but well-intentioned friend, "how good are you at dunking?"

5

Baron walked over to the basketball game and picked up the pile of tickets, which were still covered in blood/tomato sauce.

He wrapped them around his neck like a sweet scarf and slammed a token into the machine.

"Welcome to *Basketbrawl City*, where it's dunk or die!" the game shrieked in a warbled robot voice.

"Dunk!" Baron answered back.

Four basketballs shot out and flew through the air toward Baron and Garindax. In midflight, each ball split in half, revealing rows of conical fangs.

Baron grabbed Garindax's whammy bar and started wailing on it, and Garindax sprang into action.

He grew out his razor-wire strings like crazy vines and grabbed the basketballs from the sky.

The balls squirmed and chomped on the strings, but each bite shot them full of 100 volts (or more in case that's not a lot).

He continued growing them all the way up to the hoop, then slammed the balls through the net while Baron screamed quotes from *NBA Jam:*

"*Jams it in!*"

"*Boomshakalaka!*"

"*He's heating up!*"

"*He's on fire!*"

The net exploded in super patriotic red, white, and blue flames, and *Basketbrawl City* groaned in defeat.

"You dudes are truly the Dukes of Dunk," the machine coughed before vomiting up another thousand tickets.

Baron didn't even acknowledge the compliment because he already knew it to be true. Instead, he grabbed the tickets off the ground and wrapped them around Garindax's guitar neck so they both could have sweet scarves.

The Dukes of Dunk then headed over to the redemption area to spend their newfound fortune.

A pimply young geek sat behind the ticket counter playing a videogame on his phone. Baron recognized from the music that it was *Escape from Sideburn Mountain 4: In Space.*

"Oh, nice, is that *EFSM 4?*" he asked.

"First off, it's ESM, not 'EFSM,'" the geek sighed, emphasizing "EFSM" in a mockingly baby-ass voice.

Baron bristled.

"And, no," he continued, "it's *ESM 5: Sideburn Mountain in the Hood.* You probably haven't heard of it. It's pre-alpha, invite-only."

Baron saw the phone's screen reflected in the glass counter, and the nerd was definitely playing *EFSM 4*—Baron recognized the level and everything. The fact that the geek would lie about something so trivial in order to seem cool/superior made Baron's blood boil.

"Whatever, pencil-neck," Baron growled. "Just give me the best prize I can get for two thousand tickets: jetpack, radioactive scorpion, whatever. And be quick about it."

"Ha! Two *thousand?*" the geek laughed nasally. "Even this crappy rubber spider is 18 *million* tickets. Hey, it kind of looks like your guitar, doesn't it? Chinese, cheap, and crappy."

Baron and Garindax instantly/simultaneously went ballistic.

Garindax filled his fangs with his most necrotoxic venom as Baron thrust him straight at the dweeb's five-inches-in-circumference throat.

A bright flash erupted, and Garindax's fangs felt like they had just bitten into an electric Hot Pocket. His eight eyes adjusted to find the nerd still sitting behind the counter, douchely playing *EFSM 4*.

"Gold force field, motherfuckers" he sneered. "100 bojojillion tickets."

The duo's hearts sank and they choked back pizza vom in utter devastation. Not only would they have to dunk for infinity to earn enough tickets for LB's gift, but they had been bested by a dweeby hipster baby bitch.

It was the worst day in history for anyone, ever.

"Wow," Baron repeated as he walked away from the ticket counter. "I think this is it, man. I think this is finally it. Set your fangs to *seppuku.*"

Garindax's spider eyes filled with glow-in-the-dark tears, but he complied.

He and Baron had talked about this scenario numerous times, especially when they were drunk, but he never thought it would actually happen.

"If that's what you want, dude," Garindax said sadly as he extended his fangs.

"It's not what I want," Baron snapped. "It's what has to be done. For our honor. For our pump."

"I know, I know. Gotta stay pumped...Hey! 'Stay Pumped Marshmallow Man!' I just got that."

"Ha," Baron laughed, appreciating his buddy—warts and all—for the last time.

"It's been awesome knowing you, man."

"And you, dude."

Baron turned Garindax toward his chest and prepared to enter Pumphalla, which is a lot like Valhalla but with more warriors spinning in office chairs and banging on pots and pans.

6

"*Wait!*"

Baron heard the voice from across PizzArea 64. It came from a cool-looking kid holding a cooler-looking cat.

"Baron, don't do it!" the kid yelled as she ran over to the suicidal superdudes.

Garindax retracted his fangs.

Baron lowered him and said, "Make it quick, kid. We have a date with the Pump Reaper. Cool cat, by the way."

"Thanks, doods," the cat replied in a sweetly obnoxious voice. He was shock orange, overweight, wearing shades, and breathing through his mouth for some reason. Maybe he had a deviated septum, or maybe it was just preference. Either way, he looked/sounded awesome.

"Don't do it, Baron," the kid repeated. Something must've been wrong with her septum, too, because she was out of breath after running like 50 feet.

"Look, don't ask me how I know," she wheezed, "but you have so many sweet 'ventures ahead of you."

"No crap? How do you know?"

"C'mon, man, I *just* said don't ask."

"Oh, right. Sorry. I forgot."

"It's cool. I know about the ADHD."

Baron stared down at Garindax's frets, wondering what they were made of and if changing the material would make a tonal difference, or if it was more of a height thing.

"Listen, Baron," the kid continued. "You gotta trust me on this. You're needed in this realm—and in others."

Baron couldn't see through the cat's shades, but he somehow sensed the feline wink.

"But what about the geekazoid, and our pump/honor?"

"Dude, fuck that little dweeb," the kid replied sternly. "He's probably just mad because he saw you dunk so hard. He knows he'll never be able to dunk, or make out with a babe, or anything. He hates everyone because he hates himself, and that's why someday he'll die, still working *here*, a miserable old non-grandpa."

Baron thought about all the times he had dunked and made out with babes, and how it was impossible to imagine the nerd even doing a lay-up or slapping five with a chick.

The kid's logic checked out.

"Alright, homie," Baron replied. "I believe you. We'll stick around a little longer. But first…"

Baron turned and shot a middle finger to the nerd, who acted like he didn't see it. But he did, and it stung so hard he immediately game-overed and the high score screen auto-inputted "SUX."

"Fart yeah," the kid laughed.

The cat started to purr.

Garindax tried to purr, too, but it sounded really weird/off. He changed the subject before anyone noticed.

"If we're not doing the group suicide," he said, "which I'm totally down for either way, we'll still need to figure out a present for Little Billy."

"Damn. True," Baron nodded. He looked to the kid. "Got ideas?"

"Actually, yeah. I heard some poop-faced baby crying over at Looter's Lost and Found. He said he dropped a pocketknife somewhere in the ball pit."

"*Legiiiiit!*" Baron shouted as he grabbed Garindax and dashed over to the ball pit. He dove in headfirst, and with a vortical *WOOSH!* everything went black.

Baron awoke to find himself lying on the ground, staring up at a hot pink sky. Flying eyeball monsters drifted lazily below chartreuse clouds and even chartreusier stars.

"Garindax, are you okay?" Baron choked.

"Yeah, man," Garindax replied from somewhere nearby. "Pump readings nominal."

"Nominal? That's not very pumped."

Baron sat up.

"Whoa, nelly!" Garindax yelled. "Pump readings now at 4,129. What'd you see?!"

Baron picked Garindax off the ground and assumed a power stance.

Before them stood a black metal (material) gate with black metal (music) letters that read:

WELCOME TO MONSTEROPOLIS

7

After the intro credits rolled, Baron and Garindax threw open the gate and busted into World 1-1.

Spooky chiptunes faded in as the duo entered a labyrinthine pumpkin patch.

All of the pumpkins, trees, and dead grass bits were blacklit and glowing like crazy.

Baron's pump meter flashed to indicate that it was maxed out and in danger of overloading, but Garindax's remained at 93% since he still felt a twinge of embarrassment from the purring incident. Not wanting his buddy's pump to drop any further, Baron sheathed Garindax and began exploring.

He quickly noticed that as he walked deeper into the patch, fewer pumpkins and more jack-o-lanterns surrounded him. Their eyehole flames silently followed, making his arm hairs dance around like crazy.

To break the tension and determine whether the jack-o's were cool or not, Baron asked, "Yo, pumpkins, have you seen a pocketknife around here?"

"Yeah, mang," replied an oblong gourd. "Mrs. Bones ran by with one a few minutes ago. She said something about using it to 'fix us' since we were 'too scary' for her precious babies."

"*Fuuuuck* that!" Baron replied disgustedly. The pumpkins were definitely cool, and definitely in trouble.

"Don't worry, dark dudes," he assured them. "We won't let anyone make you family-friendly."

"More like family-*wimpy*," Garindax called from behind Baron.

A few pumpkins screamed because they hadn't realized he was there, but none of them laughed because they weren't fake and it wasn't funny.

"So, where's Mrs. Bones now?" Baron asked in part because he was interested but mostly to pull Garindax's frets out of the fire.

"At the edge of the patch," the jack-o's responded. "That-a-way!"

Their candles glowed neon green, which looked so rad against the blacklights that Baron got goosepumps. Ghostbumps. RL STINE.

Baron and Garindax followed the glowing trail. After about an hour ADHD-time, three minutes normal-time, they noticed another change in the jack-o monsters: this time for the worse.

The carvings featured fewer glowering eyes and sharp fangs, and more eyelashes and surprised little "*oo*" mouths.

Baron trudged ahead, putting on a forced autist smile to not let the jack-o's know how lame they looked. He palm-muted Garindax because he knew he wouldn't be able to keep his spider mouth shut.

But the pumpkins only went from worse to worst.

They became bedazzled with cheap crystals, their orange flesh poxed by glittery beauty marks and cliché phrases like "KEEP CALM AND BE A FIERCE HALLOWEENISTA" and "TRICK OR #PSL."

The most unfortunate souls weren't carved at all, but merely/crudely painted to look like the princess or snowman character from an animated movie made by a very litigious company.

These not-even-jack-o's looked *so* baby ass that it alliteratively boiled Baron's blood and ground Garindax's gears.

"Mrs. Bones will pay for this," Baron vowed as he slammed his eyes shut to avoid looking further upon the depressing harvest.

He blindly continued his journey, walking for miles and leaving a graveyard of mercy-crunched pumpkins in his wake. He would've kept walking/crunching for even *more* miles, but a stucco wall stopped him right in the face.

Baron opened his eyes to find the wall attached to a generic, two-story suburban house.

It was barely decorated, despite the fact that it's always Halloween in Monsteropolis.

One tissue paper ghost hung from a tree on the front lawn, and the porch light had been replaced with a green bulb. But that was *it*.

Meanwhile, tubs of Christmas decorations had been dragged to the side of the house, suggesting that the owner couldn't wait to take down the lone ghost at 12:00 AM on November 1 (if November 1 ever came to Monsteropolis, which it didn't).

Baron was fucking livid.

He stomped up to the porch and was about to use his jet boots to fire-kick the place to pieces, when he noticed a bowl of Halloween candy by the front door.

A sign above it read: "TAKE ONLY ONE. – MRS. BONES."

"Oh, dang!" Baron gasped. "Looks like we found Mrs. Bones. And maybe she isn't so terrible after all."

Even if a "take one" policy is stingy AF, and the underlining was a bit much, Mrs. Bones had at least put out *some* candy. Better yet, none of it was organic bullshit.

Baron felt guilty for prejudging the skeleton mom but proud that he had learned a valuable lesson.

"Garindax, whushoo want?"

"Uh, lemme get one of those unlabeled black-and-orange ones."

"The fucking *ped candies?!* No way, man! You'll get poisoned/touched for sure."

"Haha, I know, I know. JK," Garindax laughed, even though he was anything but JK. "I was just seeing if *you* knew. Hit me with a Krack-l."

"Shit, now that's more like it. I'm going Buttafinga."

Baron grabbed the two candies—exactly one for each of them.

As soon as his hand left the bowl, the front door exploded into a billion shards of faux-fancy fiberglass as he and Garindax were blasted off the porch by a vicious mom-howl:

"NOOO!!! TAKE ONLY ONE!!!"

8

It was Mrs. Bones.

Eight feet tall with four arms of terror, the crabby skeleton mom towered above Baron and Garindax.

Her apron, emblazoned with a calligraphic "Momster Knows Best," blew violently in the suburban night air. The blonde bob on her skull didn't move at all, though, since it was too short. She told everyone she cut it that way to be fashionable, but they knew she had just become lazy with age.

Baron pulled himself and Garindax off the lawn and looked up at the mini-boss who stood before them. His glance caught her narrowed eye sockets, and he was suddenly overcome with the despair of the countless kids whom she had grounded for absolutely no reason.

Only her voice broke the spell.

"Can't you READ?!" she shrieked. "TAKE ONLY ONE!"

"I *did*, you boney bag of bitch," Baron grunted while dusting himself off. He unwrapped the Buttafinga and slammed it into his mouth.

"And so did he."

Mrs. Bones looked at Baron, who was angrily chomping on his candy. Then she looked at Garindax, who was gnawing on his still-wrapped Krack-l.

She ran the numbers in her head.

Still unconvinced, she pulled out a bedazzled pink Blackberry, which she called her "iPhone" and which permanently had a shattered screen. After logging into Skullbook and sharing a few dozen memes featuring pixelated minions yelling something ungrammatical about coffee/wine, she opened a calculator app and confirmed that—in fact—1 and 1 equaled 2.

They equaled two no matter how many times she ran the calculation. Even Googling "if 1 candy for 1 but 2 how many candys.com?" didn't give her the answer she wanted. But never wanting to admit she was wrong about anything, she quickly deflected.

"Err, too bad!" she screamed. "You're too old to take ANY candy! NOW BEAT IT!"

She leapt at Baron, scratching the air with her gnarly press-on nails.

Baron deftly dodged the attack, and Mrs. Bones crashed into the ground and immediately started sobbing even though Baron hadn't done *anything* to her, and *she* was the one trying to hurt *him*.

"I…I have too much to do today," she wailed. "I'm…I'm tired…"

"Oh, fartknockers," Garindax whispered to Baron. "Dude, her pissed/pumped readings are off the charts."

Mrs. Bones realized no one was coming to her aid, so she shut off the waterworks and went back into full rage mode.

"What are we talking?" Baron replied.

"She's at a 12—no, 13."

"That's not that bad."

"Remember the mom at the frozen yogurt place in the mall? The one who went fucking *ballistic* on you after you took 'too many napkins' from the dispenser, even though it was an accident and you neatly set them off to the side?"

Baron shivered.

"She was a 4."

"Oh, fartknockers..."

Baron steadied himself and assumed a defensive power stance of maximum intensity.

"I...don't...NEED THIS RIGHT NOW!" Mrs. Bones roared, launching a stink-vortex of nail polish, nail polish remover, and perfume samples out of her diet-cola-stained mouth.

Even Baron's most powerful power stance was no match for that caliber of stink.

He and Garindax were blasted backward across the front lawn. They slammed into the tree and likely would've died on impact had the tissue paper ghost not cushioned the blow.

Baron gave it a thumbs-up, and Garindax slowly blinked at it in case tissue paper ghosts were like cats.

Mrs. Bones growled in frustration and reached into her apron.

"Baron, the knife!" Garindax shouted.

The skeleton mom had withdrawn an ancient pocketknife. It looked incredible, like something a grandpa would keep tucked away in a shoebox for decades before lovingly passing it down to his idiot grandson who would lose it in a ball pit the very same day.

Before Baron could respond/get pumped, Mrs. Bones opened the knife and lunged.

"I TOLD YOU TO CLEAN YOUR ROOM BEFORE THE MAID GETS HERE. HOW IS SHE SUPPOSED TO CLEAN IT WHEN IT'S SO MESSY?!"

Her riddle paralyzed Baron and Garindax, who became sitting/stabbable ducks.

As Mrs. Bones began her deadly descent, a small bedazzled pumpkin rolled over and vine-leapt into the sky. It looked down at Baron, gave him a knowing smile, and mouthed, "Fucking do it. I can't live this way another second. Please…set me free."

Baron's confusion was quickly replaced by compassion—and piss/pump.

He winked out a tear and swung Garindax like a baseball bat, smashing the pumpkin into a typhoon of gourd meat and cheap Barfovski crystals.

Every piece of pumpkin shrapnel blasted Mrs. Bones across her face and bone-boobs.

The pocketknife fell from the skelemom's hand and directly into Baron's as she busted infinity flips into the stratosphere.

Baron used the knife to wail a triumphant power slide on Garindax while the entire jack-o-lantern crowd cheered like crazy and flashed every color of the spooky rainbow (purple, green, orange, and blacklight [which is different than purple]).

The crew partied hard for the next few hours, eating all of Mrs. Bones' candy and taking turns pissing on her "take one" sign.

When the partying and pissing finally subsided, Baron realized that he and Garindax needed to get their newfound gift back to Little Billy before his birthday ended.

"Yo, pump-buds," Baron said with a mouthful of his 296th Buttafinga. "How do we get back to Urth from here?"

"Urth?" belched a fat jack-o monster.

"What that means?" squeaked another.

"You know, Urth. The planet or dimension or whatever that we teleported from?"

All of the pumpkins tilted on the blacklit grass, looking like a patch of confused dog heads.

"Well, fucknockers, Garindax," Baron groaned. "It looks like we're stuck here."

9

Baron ran back down the trail and past the gate, hoping the portal would still be visible/open.

It wasn't/wasn't.

He jumped around and turned over a bunch of rocks in case the portal had just become super tiny or shy, but it was nowhere to be found.

"Dude, we're gonna miss the fucking party!" Baron yelled, ignoring the fact that he had just partied for a million hours.

He felt hyper frustrated and looked for something to take it out on, which happened to be a beautifully carved cat-gourd chilling next to his feet. He picked it up and reared back a fist, ready to punchsplode it into infinity.

The tiny pumpkin shook in terror and began crying sweet-smelling pumpkin seeds.

"Yo, chill!" Garindax pleaded. He hated seeing his buddy so stressed, and he definitely didn't want to see an innocent cat-o-lantern bite the big one.

"Just take it easy, man. I understand that you're pissed about the portal—so am I. But smashing pumpkins *won't* get you re-pumped. They're way too angsty."

Baron looked over slowly.

"Eh? Eh?" Garnidax prodded. "You feeling like a rat in a cage?"

Despite all his rage, Baron chuckled at the bad joke. He un-reared his fist and morphed it into a contrite thumbs-up.

"Good, dude, good," Garindax sighed in relief. "Look, all we've eaten since we got here is fucking Halloween candy. You're prolly just hungry. Let's kill some burgs and extremepresso, and then we'll bust back. The portal will be open by then. I can feel it in my frets."

Garindax's optimism was infectious to Baron, and a burg did sound awesome.

"Alright, mang," he said. "Let's go. And thanks for talking me off the murder ledge."

He carefully set down the cat-o-lantern.

"Sorry about that, homie."

"S'okay," the pumpkin replied. "If I were trapped in an alternate dimension while a baller party was going on back home, I'd be pissed, too. I'd probably be *so* pissed, I'd punch you in the face so hard your nose would shoot out your butt and smell everything along the way."

"Dang," Baron and Garindax whispered. It was a pretty intense vision.

They chunked up a deuce on the pumpkin patch and trudged back to Mrs. Bones' house in search of meat/caffeine.

When they got there, Baron walked through where the front door had exploded, and the two entered a dark foyer.

The air reeked of expensive candles and cheap chardonnay—it was truly a mom's domain.

They cautiously busted to the kitchen, passing endless chore charts and plastic-wrapped couches. When they reached the fridge, Baron opened it hopefully.

But what he saw inside made his jaw/pump plummet through the linoleum, past the subfloor, all the way *TOOOOOOO*

THE CREEPY CRAWLSPACE.

JK JK THE SPOOKY BASEMENT.

10

"Garindax, what the fart?!" Baron thundered.

The fridge was stocked only with produce and packages labeled:

Hundo-percent non-GMO, with no chemicals you can't pronounce, which is basically everything since you majored in PoliSci at a low-tier state school with every intention of going to law school afterward because what else are you going to do with that degree, plus your dad is a lawyer and you really liked Legally Blonde when you were a kid and everyone always tells you how much you 'love to argue,' which is really just a nicer way of saying you're a disagreeable shit, but then you met someone who makes enough money so you don't have to work or pursue your education or think critically about anything other than soccer schedules and bath/bedtimes, but hey what do we know we're just applesauce.

Baron went totally ballistic. He grabbed one of the dozens of wine boxes chilling on the faux-granite island and chucked it across the room.

With a loud *PLOK-SMASH!* the box nailed a ceiling fan and burst, spraying moscato all over the rug and launching a broken fan blade right through the coffee table.

Garindax lost it, laughing so hard he made a weird snort noise that Baron had never heard before, but that made him think everything would be okay.

"Let's bail on this shit-show and find some *real* food," Baron announced as he cranked the gas on the stovetop and lit one of Mrs. Bones' countless "FOR DECORATION ONLY" candles shaped like an anthropomorphic baby Christmas tree sleeping in a manger.

As the duo stepped back outside, Mrs. Bones' house exploded so hard it actually imploded first. Stucco, vinyl, and hair scrunchies whizzed past Baron and Garindax, but not a piece touched them because they all fucking knew better.

"So, if Mrs. Bones was a mom," Garindax said as they strolled across the front lawn, "that means she has—er, *had*—kids, right? You think they were still in the house?"

A tiny skeleton hand clutching a rattle flew past Baron's head, and he and Garindax booked it in a major way.

11

After running for what seemed like infinity, Baron and Garindax found themselves at the mouth of Monsteropolis.

Literally.

Two bloated, hovering lips blocked their path. Behind them towered shadowy skyscrapers, neon highways, and misty mountains with foliage in the shape of sideburns.

As Baron approached, the purple lips trembled and curled, revealing tremendous fangs covered in frothy white slime.

"*Oooh,*" it moaned in a high, quavering voice like that of a grandpa/uncle whose lap you *never* fucking sit on.

"Why, whom do we have here? A widdle baby bard and his widdle baby strum-strum? Come to serenade us with a…mellifluous melody?

"OHFUCKNO," Baron growled as he insta-flew into a rage and flipped three pickup switches at the same time.

Garindax burped, and from his output jack spewed a hologram doppelgänger.

The hologram burped and shot out a smaller hologram, which burped and shot out a smaller hologram, which belched and vommed up a hologram smaller to the 64th power.

It was the fabled *pumpstroyshka dollogram* technique, taught to Garindax during his studies with the beautiful and mysterious Zamoldchikova of "the old country" somewhere outside Boston.

The holograms surrounded the mouth monster and looked pissed as fuck.

Rightfully impressed/terrified, it relented.

"*Oooooh*," it moaned again, this time with a couple extra *o*'s. "Please excuse my…impetuous impertinence. I did not realize you were beings of such…preeminent pumpitude. And with such…magnificent musculature."

A plop of drool oozed over the mouth's bottom lip, causing Baron's neck hairs to stand up in anything but a cool way.

"Let us pass," Garindax demanded with the confidence of someone backed by an army of his own hologram doppelgängers. "Or my homies here will punch you so hard your nose will shoot out your butt and smell everything along the way."

"*Mmm*," the monster cooed. "Promises, promises."

Now Garindax's neck hairs (dust and cat hair lodged beneath his strings) stood on end, too.

"As much as I would relish such an...odiferous outing, such a...putrid peregrination," the mouth slavered, biting its lower lip in deep thought, "I am afraid I have neither a nose to hit, nor a butt to sniff."

Garindax ran biometric scans and confirmed the monster's claims, which was a bummer since he had just wasted his cool new line on it.

The ambiguous mouth smiled kindly/creepily.

"But where *are* my manners? Please allow me to introduce myself. I am Halitosep, Esquire: gatekeeper and liaison between Monsteropolis and the Belowburbs."

"Belowburbs?" Baron asked. "The gate next to the portal we came through, like 800 miles ago, said we were already *in* Monsteropolis."

"You—and they—only wish," Halitosep sneered. "For you see, a thousand sandoodillion years ago, the throne of Samzário Spumándiosmío VIII, a most terrible, dandruffy king, was usurped—but doesn't that sound awful? Let us say 'ascended'—by our glorious, dandruff-free, present-day ruler: The Boogeyman. It was his Divine Fright, and our Monifest Destiny.

"What followed—though I and the Knights of the Boogey Board assure you is a *subsequence* and not a *consequence* of our current king's rightful, albeit perhaps…anachronistic ascendancy—became known as the 'Weak Wiener Withdrawal.'

"During this period, Monsteropolis' lowest-level inhabitants—momsters, eyeball pigeons, bipedal butt-walkers, uncarved pumpkins and any lesser…carved Cucurbitaceae—fled to the safety and seclusion of the Belowburbs.

"Though they believe they still reside in Monsteropolis—and if someone wrote 'Monsteropolis' instead of 'Belowburbs' on a piece of mail it would probably get to them—they are not us, and we are not them."

Baron started to ask if carved cupurbwhatevers were actually jack-o's, and if so what the "morer" ones were like since the "lesser" ones were already pretty sweet. But then he remembered how bored/hungry/tired he was of watching a mouth monster drool all over the place, so all that went out the frigg'n window.

"Listen, Halitoaststep," Baron snarled. "We don't give a crap about history."

"*Don't give a crap about biology...*" Halitosep sang.

"Fucking let us through. NOW."

Baron stomped forward, ready to rock. The squadron of doppelgängers everyone had forgotten about followed, also ready to rock.

"What will you give me if I do?" Halitosep asked, licking its purple lips with an even purpler tongue.

"How about a busted fat *EVERYTHING?*"

Baron wielded Garindax and jet-booted into the sky.

Garindax used the higher vantage point and his eight spider eyes to look in all directions, hoping to catch a glimpse of a bipedal butt-walker farting its way across the foggy horizon.

On Baron's cue (a thumbs-up), the holograms began shredding in perfect unison but through various effects pedals: one was super distorted, which shot out a laser that caused rock damage; one was heavy on reverb, which blasted out a water laser; one added chorus, an air laser; and the last was a death metal effect called "JopPin joLapEño GoRAGE-NuKroLAVAble pIZZa RoLLz," which fired a laser hotter than any Thai dish—even if the restaurant's menu only goes from 1-4 spicy stars but some puffy-nipped nerdo tells the waitress "13 stars" in an attempt to impress her.

While the doppelgängers wailed, Baron king-chilled in midair, doing flips and generally looking awesome.

"Oh, my *LAAAAND!*" Halitosep yelled as the lasers slowly combined. The monster mouth knew it was screwed, but it also didn't care since this was the most exciting thing that had happened in a while.

Baron simultaneously picked the lowest and highest notes on Garindax, causing acid, ghost, ice, and school attacks to blast out of his fangs.

The quad-damage laser started partying with the doppelgängers' lasers, and all of their colors and elements merged into the Ultimate Lazer [sic/sick as fuck]. It was black or white, whatever the presence of all colors is—probably white, even though if you add every color of Easter egg dye to a glass, the water definitely turns black. But for some reason it's different for light, and lasers are closer to light than Easter egg dye.

The white/black *UltimaOctoLazer*™ slammed into Halitosep with the power of eight x-rays taken in a podiatrist's office in a strip mall in the shittiest part of town.

It scorched through the monster's lips, bubbling and popping infinity blisters before burrowing deeper into its vile gums. Every root got canaled as micro-explosions and tiny breath strips rocketed Halitosep's teeth into the sky.

The fangs missed Baron and Garindax by a nanometer before flipping and falling back toward their previous host.

"*NOEOEOEO! WAWAWA!*" Halitosep garble-shrieked as the teeth punctured it 32 ways from Sunday.

"Yo, does this monster make you feel funny, too?" Garindax whispered to Baron, who had stopped flipping to look awesome and started flipping out of boredom.

"Yeah, man," Baron replied. "Not a fan. Let's wrap it up and hope Monsteropolis' food is worth this bullshit parade."

They dropped from the sky and busted over to Halitosep, who was on the last few seconds of its game over countdown.

"Baron..." the mouth coughed through blood and slime.

"What is it, weirdo?" Baron snapped. "And how do you know my name?"

"Never you mind. To defeat King Boogey...you must—wait, what? *'Weirdo'?*"

"Yeah, you're a huge fuck' weirdo. Garindax and I had a full conversation about it, and we both agreed."

"Wow," Halitosep stammered. "Fine, just fine. I was going to help you, but now you can forget it. You...prurient pervert. You...salacious scalawag. You...big dumb jerk. I can't believe I ever loved you. *Have fun dying.*"

The mouth monster melted into a pile of puke and butt-breath vapors.

Baron didn't let on, but Halitosep's final words caused his scared/pumped ratio to creep a little closer to one.

12

Baron and Garindax bid farewell to the doppelgängers, who went off to get jobs installing cable or something, and then crossed the mush of taste buds that was Halitosep.

As they took their first steps into Monsteropolis proper, the air became heavier and reeked of fog machines, paint, and latex.

Dark glass towers and haunted subway stations lay closest on the horizon. Beyond them, asphalt streets regressed into cobblestone roads, where windows of ancient ghoul villages flickered softly in the night. In the farthest distance, where there were no roads, loomed primordial mountains whose hidden rivers and honeycombed passages teemed with blind crayfish, trolls, and troll 2's.

The possibilities were as endless as they were intense, and thinking about them caused Baron to simultaneously pop a boner and get nervous dump feeling. Once both subsided, he and Garindax continued their journey.

The blacklit highway leading downtown was lined on each side with jack-o-lanterns, and suddenly what Halitosep had said before dying made sense.

These jack-o's were infinitely tougher/"morer" than their Belowburbs cousins. They were not only bigger and orangier, but they looked like they would chomp the crap out of any skeleton mom who tried to paint or bedazzle them.

It was impossible to even *imagine* a skeleton mom in this environment, though, unless she was equally tough: like one who goes to her kids' soccer game with beer instead of moscato in a BPA-*full* thermos, queen-chills in the folding chair of another mom without even asking, and laughs at any kid who trips over the ball—even if the kid is hers and *especially* if the kid starts crying.

Anyway, Baron was pumped/impressed. Monsteropolis had brought the pump in a major way, and right off the frigg'n bat.

He assumed a power stance with Garindax and began playing an atmospheric monster ballad in homage. The song was fully instrumental and had enough spooky undertones to make it sound like something that would play in a commercial haunt, probably in an antechamber or actor-free graveyard where you could stop for a minute to smell the walls and get weirdly existential without any teenage workers chasing you away or patrons goofing on you to their hot girlfriends.

There was rarely a time when Baron wasn't pissed, pumped, or pissed/pumped, but for the moment he was also happy.

Miles away, The Boogeyman furrowed the brow beneath his crown. With the flick of a gnarled finger, an amorphous darkness emerged from behind his throne and denim-swooshed into the night.

13

After playing the last note of what had become a 75-minute interlude, Baron sheathed Garindax and continued the journey into downtown Monsteropolis.

Once there, he found himself in the heart of a bustling cityscape. Black skyscrapers obfuscated the sky, monster cabs honked, street vendors shrieked, and bus station creeps with their hands in their pockets leered at passersby.

Amongst all the chaos and nonsense, Baron spotted a diner and busted over to it.

"Welcome to Scrape the Goodie Off!" chirped a hunchback hostess as the starving duo entered. "Just one tonight?"

"2P," Baron corrected.

He nodded to Garindax, but since Garindax was slung across his back and also a guitar, he just looked like he was fucking crazy, nodding at the air and saying shit like "2P."

"You got it," the hunchback replied, unaffected because she was entirely used to crazy.

She grabbed a handful of menus and led Baron to a nearby booth.

All of the monster patrons turned their heads/eyestalks to watch him as he confidently strode by. Some looked super pumped, but others looked super pissed.

Baron ignored the latter group, as a wise fortune cookie once told him that if strangers look pissed at you, it's probably because you're so badass that it caused them to look at their own biceps, and then at yours, and then regret every decision they've ever made—including/especially the first day of middle school when they gelled their hair super flat and loudly proclaimed it "gerbil hair" in front of the entire class.

He was also too hungry to give a crap.

"A waitress will be right with you, uh, boys," the hunchback hostess said as Baron and Garindax crashed into their booth and she turned to walk back to the front.

"Hey, wait," Baron stopped her. "What does 'Scrape the Goodie Off' even mean?"

"Oh. It means when you scrape the goodie off. Like, when you scrape off all the goodie."

"What the fart kind of answer is that?!" Baron sputtered.

The hunchback smiled, shrugged her hunch, and retreated back to her station.

As soon as she left, a tangerine slug waitress slimed over to the booth.

Peeking/jiggling over the apron plastered to her belly was a pair 36-X slug boobs, prominently displayed as a way of helping her earn bigger tips to feed her little slug babies at home.

"Evenin', suga's!" she said in a hybrid accent that was part Creole, part Sluganese. "What can I get y'all?"

"What've you got?" Baron barked.

Garindax swallowed hard because the obvious answer was *big fat planet-sized slug jugs.*

"Aw, you po' 'literate thang," the waitress said, taking Baron's crunginess (crabby/hungriness) as a sign that he couldn't read the menu.

She bent over to point to various items.

Baron knew better than to stare into the sun, but Garindax took the bait.

His eight eyes hyperfocused and he became hypnotized, pupils lightly dancing and swaying in time with the bulbous subject of their reflection.

"We got brains in a cup," the waitress pointed, "booga's by the bowl, spida' egg soufflé, eyelash-stuffed ravioli in plum sauce, baby bird beaks on toast, and—today only—our KB Special."

Baron chose the special since it was the last thing the waitress mentioned and he had a super short attention span.

Garindax blurted out "blue bubblegum snowcone" because it was all he could think to say other than "slug jug soufflé a la jigglé."

The waitress wrote down both orders and left, leaving Garindax feeling pumped that maybe blue bubblegum snowcones were a secret menu item, and now she would be impressed/turned on by the fact that knew about them. Or even if they *weren't* a secret menu item, maybe she dug him so much that she would personally make him one, and include at the bottom of the cone a mini-SD card loaded with pics/vids of her slug jugs organized into folders by outfit, lighting, and slime glisten.

Before he could continue down that rabbit hole, the metal kitchen doors exploded open and a crazed, obese chef monster stormed into the dining room wielding two meat cleavers.

Déjàfuckvu.

14

"*Awwwwwhl-RAYHT!*" a voice seemed to yell, even though the chef's mouth didn't move. "Who heah orda' mah KB Speshah?!"

Baron slowly but super confidently stood up, fret fingers at the ready.

"Yo," he growled. "Sup."

"Syrup?!" the chef seemed to shout, his eyes rolling around in his head. He shambled toward Baron's booth.

All of the monster patrons in the diner watched intensely.

"What the bitch are you talking about?" Baron garbled, as he was battling a depumpbilitating mix of confused/pissed/hungry. "And how are you talking about *anything* without moving your mouth?"

"Wha', thas nah mah mouf!" the chef said while shaking and pointing at his bloated rosacea dome. "Dis heah mah mouf!"

He pulled aside his greasy apron and ripped open his greasier shirt. Where his belly button should've been, there was a hideous rictus.

It twisted into a smile and shrieked, "*An' dis mah KAAAYBEEEE SPESHAH!*"

The mouth/chef's stomach split wide open, and a quintoxillion putrid earwigs and soft-shell crabs spilled across Baron and Garindax's table.

Baron insta-vommed, coating the fetid spread in chunks of Buttafinga and bile.

"*Oh, ho, HO!*" the chef laughed. "An' dere's yah syrup!"

Baron reeled and fell back into the booth.

Vomming on an already-empty stomach had left him too hungry to deliver another ass beating, even though the chef needed it bad.

Garindax knew that the onus fell upon his frets. He unwound his low E and A strings and wailed a quick power chord riff on the remaining four.

Ice crystals slowly formed on the chef's apron, but they were immediately shaken off.

"So, yah lahk myusahk, do yah?!" the monster chuckled. He motioned to the hunchback hostess, who punched a jukebox by the entrance. "Ah lahk myusahk, too! Les boogah!"

Monster doo-wop began pulsing into the diner. A vampire, who sounded more Jewish or Jamaican than Transylvanian, crooned:

In the still of the night!
I gave you, gave you a bite!
'Cause I love, love blood so!
Promise you'll never stop the flow!
In the still of the night!

It was a lazy-as-fuck parody, but it managed to drown out the rest of Garindax's attacks.

He and Baron were completely helpless—and at the mercy of the super-original obese chef/mouth monster with a tattoo of a skeleton mom on his left bicep.

15

Right before Baron and Garindax succumbed to the growing tide of earwigs, crabs, and vom, the chef's stomach-mouth shot out a buffalo chicken pizza with buffalo chicken pizza bagels on top. And then, a blue bubblegum snowcone the size of a basketball on a traffic cone.

"Garindax…" Baron muttered on the brink of starvation. "Are you seeing this, too…or is it some kind of fuck' mirage?"

Before Garindax could respond, the chef did.

"Nah meerah', frand! Da' dere's da goodah!"

"What…what the fuck…is goodie…"

"Goodah whah ya scrape ahf!"

The chef spiked a spatula into Vom Mountain, turned, and walked back into the kitchen.

The monster patrons turned their attention back to their meals, again filling the diner with the sounds of silverware clinks and satisfied grunts.

Baron and Garindax stared at each other, totally bewildered.

They hesitantly grabbed the spatula, scraped the 'za and snowcone onto their plates, and took a cautious first bite.

"The puke is gross as fuck," Baron said after some deliberation, "but the 'za is good as fuck."

"Same," Garindax replied. "But 'snowcone' for the second part, not 'za.'"

The two ate in silence for a bit.

"I guess that's what they mean, huh?" Baron eventually remarked.

"About what?"

"'Scrape the Goodie Off.' Like, scrape off all the good stuff? Leave the shitty stuff behind?"

"I guess so."

"Then why not 'Scrape the Shitty Off'?"

"Maybe they're going for a family vibe."

"Well, then 'Scrape the *Grossy* Off.' It's all the same. You're scraping vom off whatever you want to eat. And there's way more bad stuff than good."

"I guess they're choosing to focus on the pump instead of the slump."

Baron felt a twinge of guilt, and the two went back to eating in silence.

After finishing their meals, the duo dropped some cash on the table and booked it before the waitress came back just in case Monsteropolis diners didn't take Urth money.

Back outside and fully re-pumped/re-primed, they decided to head back to the Belowburbs and see if the portal had re-opened.

It was possible that it hadn't, and it was equally possible that Little Billy's party would be over even if it had.

Regardless, they needed to try. They had to stay pumped. They had to scrape the goodie off.

But as soon as Baron stepped into the street, a vine ensnared his mountainous trapezius muscles and a shrill voice rasped, "*Hello, BABY!*"

16

Baron spun around and found himself face-to-plant with a Venus flytrap prostitute monster.

Her flytrap lips were artificially plumped with chlorophyll and painted bright red, and the trigger hairs lining the inside of her mouth were pierced and sessily coiffed. Her stem was bare, her curvy bulb packed tightly into patent leather, and each of her dozen roots wore a stiletto boot.

"Whoa..." Baron said as his newly popped boner slammed into her and projected himself backward.

Her vines reached out and ensnared him, pulling him close again.

"Where ya headed, baby?" she asked. Her mouth made a super annoying clapping sound with each word, and her breath smelled like mummified flies.

Baron's boner/pump deflated.

“We’re headed to an awesome party back on Urth,” Baron snarled, “and you’re not invited.”

“C’mon, baby,” the VFPM moaned, slapping a vine into Baron’s crotch, which she thought would be hot but actually just hurt.

“I like to party, too. How you want to party with me? Table shower? Tombstone powerhouse pumpkin-blumpkin? Get your guitar in on it, have a couples’ tombstone powerhouse pumpkin-blumpkin with a nightmare ending?”

“I don’t know what any of that bullshit is,” Baron replied, “but I imagine it’ll make me all red and itchy. So, pass.”

She tightened her vine-grip around Baron’s peen, and her stem grumbled in hunger.

“*Ooh, baby,*” she sighed, her drooling maw opening wide. “Just slam that ping-pong between these leaves and let cha’ girl dissolve it…”

“What the fuck?! No! And stop calling me baby. I *hate* babies.”

Baron twisted her vines into a giant knot and punched them like a tetherball. It slammed into the prostie’s mouth, and she instinctively clapped shut and began digesting her own arms.

“*Hrmph!*” she gagged while flailing around the street and disappointing her parents.

"Hasn't anyone told you that it's rude to talk with your mouth *chlorofull?*" Baron chuckled. "Chlorofilled? I dunno. Yo, Garindax, you know what to do."

"Yeah, man," Garindax replied. "I'm on it."

He had absolutely no idea what to do.

Never wanting to disappoint, though, he started humming and waving a couple of strings around.

Out of nowhere, a City of Monsteropolis garbage truck careened down the street and slammed into the VFPM, leaving behind a grease stain comprising the pollen of 37 dude plants.

"Beauty!" Baron cheered. "Good job, man. All I needed was help picking the better pun, but shit."

He petted Garindax's pickups.

"Anytime," Garindax replied, totally confused but happy to get the pets.

The garbage truck screeched to a halt. The driver, a beer-bellied troll with greased-back hair and greased-on wifebeater, rolled down his window and in a New Jersian accent yelled, "Hey! Tha' fug is goin' on ova' heah?!"

"You just ran over a Venus flytrap prostitute monster and it was all your fault," Baron replied, shifting the blame in case the driver wasn't cool.

But he definitely *was* cool.

"Ha!" the troll snorted, causing his beer belly to jiggle and gold necklace to clang.

"A VFPM, eh? Or, as we used to call 'em back at tha' docks, an ol' plant-based penis punching bag! Hoh! But, hey, no matta'! Jus' leave it to a gahbage monsta' to take out a bit a' gahbage!"

He threw a switch in the truck and the dumping bed raised.

Two tons of acid garbage sludge spilled onto the street. It looked/smelled awesome, like radioactive pecan pie guts.

Baron shredded a thrash solo as the municipal waste dissolved the VFPM grease stain.

While Baron played, the garbage monster wailed air guitar and rocked out hard, kicking his steering wheel and honking the horn kind of off-time with the solo, but it was okay because it was done with unadulterated, fully-pensioned pump.

As Baron infini-bent the final note, the garbage monster slammed a cigar into his mouth and ashed it in one puff. He gave a thumbs-up, spun out his tires for a minute, and blazed off into the night while shouting, "Fuckin' metal all tha' way!"

Baron watched the truck's blacklight taillights fade into the darkness.

He thought about how awesome it would've been if that dude had been his dad.

How awesome it would've been if *anyone* had been his dad.

"You okay, man?" Garindax asked.

Baron stared into the inky sky.

Orange clouds and eyeball vultures solemnly cruised by against a backdrop of lonely blood stars and social anxiety gore planets.

17

"Baron! Fucking wake up!"

Baron's eyes shot open. He was still staring up at the sky, only now he was on his back and his head hurt like a mug on a Monday.

"Whoa..." he muttered. "What the fart happened? Must've crashed out."

He backflipped up and noticed that he was lighter than he should have been.

Garindax wasn't there.

"At your six, man!" his buddy called from somewhere. "Your two? Eighteen? Frigg'n look out!"

Baron turned just in time for his jaw to catch a mailbox-sized fist. He twisted and flew through the air, slamming down hard before finding himself staring at the sky again.

"Har har har—*WAK WAK WAK!*" a deep voice laughed. "Do a barrel roll!"

Baron tried flipping up again, but his right arm was wrecked. He ate dirt.

"Wuh-wuh-wing damage!" the voice taunted.

Since he couldn't flip, Baron stood up like a normal dude, but a normal dude who was fully pissed/primed.

He turned to face his new archrival: a stout, barrel-chested caveman monster wearing jean *EVERYTHING*—hat, shirt, jacket, pants, shoes, shoelaces, you-name-it.

Baron swallowed hard upon the realization that he was dealing with a true maniac. But then he saw that the caveman held Garindax in a denim anti-pump web, so he spit hard instead.

"Have a good nap?" the caveman chuckled.

"You're fuck' dead!" Baron yelled so intensely that his voice cracked, so "dead" sounded more like "day-eed" or maybe even "dad." It was brutal, but he couldn't help it. Seeing Garindax confined stressed him out, plus his throat was mega dry since he had just woken up, plus stuff like that happens to *everyone* at some point so it shouldn't be a big deal.

But it was to the caveman.

"Har har, oh my fuck," he gasped. "I can't handle it. The way I heard you busted into

Monsteropolis, I thought you were going to be *tough*. But now I see you're nothing but a little baby bitch—a little baby Bichon, actually. Chilling in an old grandma's purse, smelling like butterscotch and spearmint. Shameful. Anyway, King Boogey needs your guitar. He also needs you to stop fucking around with all our citizens. *Suh-suh-suh see ya, idiot!*"

The caveman slung a hoverboard (a real one, not a bullshit one) off his back, grabbed Garindax by the neck (which should never be done to a guitar), and took off going 6,507 miles per second.

Baron sat on the ground and wondered what the fuck just happened.

He had never felt so depressed and powerless. He wanted to melt or disintegrate or explode something. Even himself. Especially himself.

Suddenly, a hamburger-shaped constellation formed in the cosmos, and an ethereal voice bellowed, "GET PUMPED OR DIE TRYING."

It was Pump Prophecy 3:16.

Baron furrowed his eyebrows so hard they tickled his nostrils. He shouted super deeply (but not in an overcompensating way) and used his good arm to do a pushup-handstand-flip, launching himself into the sky where he grabbed a pair of eyeball vultures to stay afloat.

An ordinary/weaker man would've become distracted because they felt like boobs, but Baron remained hyper-focused. He spanked the eyeball vultures to make them flap their leathery wings faster and then quickly blazed after his best friend.

18

After remembering that he was wearing jet boots, Baron ditched the eyeball vultures and quickly followed the hoverboard's chemtrail to Monsteropolis Community College.

He found the caveman chilling behind a gym, kneeling carefully to avoid getting grass stains on his denim everything and awkwardly trying to play Garindax for a succubus cheerleader.

"Sh'yeah, babe," the caveman said, plunking the same two chords (E and Em) over and over. He sounded a lot different talking to the chick than when he talked crap to Baron. His voice was way higher, and each sentence had an unconfident question intonation.

"After my internship with the Knights of the Boogey Board is finished, Dean the Beanhead and I are totally starting a band? It's going to be, like, a death metal instrumental thing? But with, like, a progressive electroswampsynth vibe?"

"Oh, Maniac Johnny," the succubus swooned. "You're so cool, and your face is so symmetrical."

"Sh'yeah, *and?*"

"And I love that you have an internship with the government, so even though you're in a metal band now, once you graduate you can wear salmon polos and buy me an entry-level luxury SUV. I'll need one to drive our bowl-cut babies to tai chi, which they'll call 'tai chi latte' because I'll always order a chai tea latte before taking them."

"No doubt, babe, but what *else?*"

"And—I just *love* the way your denim rustles!"

"Sh'yeah, there it is," Johnny said contently. He dropped Garindax and began arrhythmically thrusting/rustling.

Garindax was relieved to get a break from the caveman trying to play him, and super relieved that he fell face down so he wouldn't have to see the denim thrustles. Unfortunately, he could still hear them.

"I'm hoping to mic my den' when we play our first gig?" Johnny continued. "And, like, really make sure it sounds solid on all the monitors?"

Garindax began to eat dirt in hopes that it had a low LD50.

The succubus scooted closer to the caveman. "Totally. That'd be so hot. Say, Johnny, do you think *I* could be in your band?"

"Ooh, I dunno, babe," Johnny replied cavalierly. "That's a toughie. What can you play, other than *denim flute?*" He wiggled his fingers at his crotch and intensified the thrustling.

"Well, nothing," she giggled. "But I bet I can sing! I'm probably really good at it."

"I could see that. Your throat's pretty banging. So, uh, I dunno, sh'yeah? I'm sure DtBh won't mind. Maybe instead of instrumental metal, we could do like a chill folk thing instead?"

Baron had heard enough. He dropped out of the sky directly on top of the chick, squishing her into a pancake topped with pom-pom berries.

Blood and succubus juices (Long Island iced tea, mostly) sprayed all over Maniac Johnny, but not a droplet touched Garindax—Baron made sure of that.

The caveman monster shot to his feet, creating a sonic boom of denim.

"*BRO, my chick!* You squashed my chick!" he yelled, his voice cracking big time as he fluctuated between tough voice and baby voice.

"My guitar and best friend! You stole my guitar and best friend!" Baron mimicked using the babier version of Johnny's voice, but still refusing to say "bro."

"Heh heh, so good," Garindax snickered into the dirt.

"Right, I guess I did, huh?" Johnny said coldly. "Well, then, now we're even."

He lifted Garindax from the ground, raised a knee, and brought him down hard. Even Garindax's neck of twisted nails was no match for Maniac Johnny's knee of woven denim.

There was a sickening snap—then silence.

Baron's heart dropped into his boots, burrowed through them, and kept going until it reached Monsteropolis' version of China.

All of the Chinese monsters were so struck by the heart's sadness that they sang songs and told stories about it for generations, but due to what scientists/preschool teachers have dubbed the "telephone effect," within weeks everyone was crying over a mythical earthworm warrior who killed his dog after failing to catch it on a marshmallow pillow.

19

Baron rushed to Garindax's side.

"Busted!" the caveman monster laughed. "Like, actually busted. In half. He dead."

Baron morphed every molecule of his body into pure, fiery hate, and jet-boot launched himself at Maniac Johnny.

He torched through the denim like a crazy lava arrow. The flesh went even easier.

As Baron blazed through Johnny's torso, he started chomping all over the place, taking out chunks of flesh/heart/bone until his head, covered in blood like a crazed vulture, exploded through the other side.

Baron then swung his knees down, smashing the caveman in the crotch and exploding any chance he ever had of polluting the world with little denim babies.

Johnny shriek-barfed with such force that it blasted Baron out of his chest cavity. He stuck a perfect landing, covered in blood, puke, and pump.

But it was a hollow victory.

He rushed over to Garindax, who was dying (or "frying eggs" as Baron called it to help mitigate the pain/reality of the situation).

"Dude!" Baron cried as he frantically picked up the two pieces that were once his best friend in the universe.

"Syrup," Garindax choked.

"Oh, man, nice callback," Baron replied.

"Heh. You know it," Garindax rasped. "Anyway, I think I'm out."

"No way, José," Baron said with a smile.

Garindax gave him a confused look.

"Callback," Baron urged.

"Really?"

"Yeah. Remember? The first chef monster?"

"Nah, not really. But, crap, man, *first* chef monster. Today was pretty sweet, huh?"

"Big time," Baron said, running his fingers over Garindax's frayed and broken strings—they were beyond tuning.

The duo sat in silence as Garindax's breathing became less labored, and less frequent.

"Goodnight, my precious homie," Baron whispered.

"Ugh, frigg'n weird," Garindax replied while narrowing his spider eyes at Baron.

Baron started to chuckle, but he stopped when the eight orbs faded from blacklight to straight black.

For hours, Baron wept like he didn't give a crap—because he didn't. The tears washed away the blood, the pain, and the past.

He had just experienced the biggest drop on the most blackout pump rollercoaster of his life, and now the first incline lay ahead of him. He'd have to crest it if he wanted to reach that sweet vertical loop.

With Garindax's parts slung over his shoulder, Baron turned toward Monsteropolis Community College.

He needed to find a necromancer.

20

Monsteropolis CC's front doors exploded open as Baron busted into the main hallway.

At first glance, it looked like a normal enough monster school. There were rusted/slimy lockers; screaming eyeball clocks; janitors wheeling mop buckets filled with guts; and countless monsters of various shapes, sizes, and coolnesses.

The nerdiest monsters, a clan of emaciated ghoul-geeks, huddled in a far corner, gnawing on bones and staring longingly at monster babes.

The babes were (de)composed of cheerleader succubae and mummies wrapped so tightly you could see their areola bumps. Each of the babes was attached at the hip, some of them literally, to a party/jock monster: swamp creatures with bleach-tipped fins and Frankenstein monsters in piecemealed varsity jackets.

Ordinary fucking monsters. I hate 'em, Baron thought.

He kept scanning until he found whom he was looking for: the goth monsters. The majority of them were baby-ass vampires wearing eyeliner and black lipstick and rocking such unconfident posture that their fangs dipped below their shoulders. The rest comprised werewolves with dyed black fur and full-finger rings, ghouls who were just cool/rich enough to not have to hang with the ghoul-geeks, and overweight zombies who weren't goth at all but merely wore black to hide their bellies.

Baron didn't see any witches or warlocks (your typical necromancers) chilling within that island of misfit monsters, so he busted over to ask where they might be.

"Hey, man," Baron said as he approached one of the cooler-looking werewolf dudes.

The werewolf looked up, narrowed his eyes, and blew a massive cloud of vape in Baron's face.

Normally, Baron would've smashed the kid's fucking face before the vape dissipated, but he needed to play it cool if he wanted Garindax back in one piece.

"Uh, thanks for the vapeshare, homie," Baron coughed.

"N.p., mon," the werewolf said in a voice that sounded like a high baby lost in a bat cave. "Great plumage on that one. It's VeeVape's latest juice, *Eldritch Taint*."

"Yeah, I can totally taste the mold," Baron said, swallowing back a rush of vom.

"Sweet, rad," the werewolf replied softly. He looked back at the ground.

"So, uh," Baron ventured, "do you know any necromancers around here?"

"Ya," the werewolf replied sleepily, while still not looking up. "I think Leila's into the 'mance. I've seen her bring back bugs and crap. Discontinued sodas. Little stuff. But it doesn't always turn out right.

"One time, she brought back Slice Red, but it wasn't in the black can. Another time she brought back a petrified belch owl. It started belching like crazy. I don't know if that's what they normally do—probably is, because their name—but the belches fucking reeked. I mean, like hot grandma egg farts. Not, like, the grandma was hot, but the farts were. So, I guess 'grandma egg hot farts.' 'Grandma hot egg farts'?"

Baron choked back another torrent of vom.

"Anyway, I was vaping my favorite juice at the time, *Covered Couch in What Is Most Likely a Haunted House Because the Clawfoot Tub in the Upstairs Bathroom Has an Octopus in It.* It's also by VeeVapes. I can write it down if you want."

"I'll remember," Baron lied.

"Sweet, rad. So, anyway, now I can't vape that flavor."

"Damn," Baron said, relieved that the gross-yet-boring story was over. "Sucks."

"Ya, it's tragic," the werewolf sighed with a dramatic hair flip. "I doubt I could even, like, vapeshare it at this point."

He said the last bit super awkwardly, so Baron got pumped thinking he had taught the werewolf a new term and now he was using it because he thought Baron was cool.

"So, where's Leila now?" Baron asked.

"Um, I think she's *in* Necromancy, ashley."

"Ashley?"

"Actually."

"Dude," Baron said, losing his patience. "What room?"

"Oh. Uh, 13-," the werewolf started before he was cut off by a vampire with hot pink bangs gelled into inverted crosses that covered both of his eyes.

"Hey, man, don't tell this poser where Leila is," the vampire whined. "He's probably a pervert. Or a cop. Heh, a perv cop poser. How repugnant."

Baron's capillaries, veins, and other blood parts filled with rage. He ran every calculation in his head to see if he could kill this kid without scaring off the werewolf (who seemed sensitive) or drawing the attention of a bunch of professor monsters. Thinking about crabby teachers yelling at him when they didn't understand the situation hit too close to home, though, and Baron just frigg'n lost it.

He grabbed the vampire's bangs and ripped them off his scalp, turned them right-side up, and slammed them back into place.

The vampire shrieked as the crosses burned through his eyelids and *Wyld I'z* cat-eye contacts, which he claimed to have bought to make him look sexier to the other goth monster dudes, but that was just a ploy to make him look sexier to the goth monster chicks.

Baron wasn't finished. He slammed Garindax's broken guitar neck into the vampire's chest and hammered it in with his pickups. The makeshift stake blasted its way through the monster's back, taking his heart along for the ride.

The vampire fell to his knees and blindly scrambled for his heart in an attempt to cram it back into place—but it was too late.

Dude was ash.

The hallway exploded into screams as monster students and adjunct professors tore around in every direction.

"Oh, crap," Baron muttered as he came back to reality from his violent catharsis.

He needed to find Leila and get out of there ASAP. All he knew was that she was in room 13-something.

He looked down the hallway.

Every room was 13-something.

Because it was a monster school.

21

Baron busted into the nearest classroom.

A skeleton sat atop an exercise bike, cranking his legs like crazy. Attached to the wheels were two wires, which terminated on the nipples of a giant bat monster.

"*Oh, do come in!*" the bat called to Baron.

But he was frigg'n out of there.

He tried the next door.

A fish monster in a polka dot dress stood at the front of the classroom. She turned abruptly at his intrusion.

"What is the meaning of this?" she demanded.

Baron scanned the room. It was full of witches, warlocks, and a few elder bog monsters. The day's assignment was written on the chalkboard:

10/31 (SHOW YOUR WORK)—
Revive each of the following:
1) Nukerowaved vomroach
2) Tropical PP sucker
3) OG Ghoul-Aid (packet, not pouch)

Baron knew he was in the right place.

"Uh," he started, picking up some papers from a nearby desk and shuffling them to look official. "The principal would like to see, uh, Leila."

"*Ooooh!*" the class erupted. They turned their gaze to the middle desk, where an insanely hot witch babe shrank in her seat.

She had pale skin, black hair, black eyeshadow, black lipstick, black nail polish, rad jugs, and a *Critters from the Commode 2* t-shirt that she wore because she dug the sequel *more* than the original, and not just because it was more obscure.

She was the kind of babe you would take to Taco Bell before busting over to Party City to look for Halloween stuff even though it's only May: a real keeper.

Baron insta-popped a boner and used the stack of papers to cover it, which meant holding them super far away.

Leila stood up and started moving toward him, when a giant fin covered in red nail polish grabbed her by the shoulder.

"Leila's not going *ANYWHERE* until I finish my lesson!" the teacher screamed, spitting bits of fish food/feces all over Baron. "Now *PARK IT*."

Baron's boner evaporated into a fine mist, and he plopped down at an empty desk.

Leila returned to hers.

"Alright, class," the teacher began, "where was I before I was so *RUDELY* interrupted? Ah, yes. Open your *Necromancynomicons* to page 138—"

"No!" Baron interrupted. "You can't tell me what to do!" He leapt out of his seat, boner insta-reboned.

"I *can't*, or I *mayn't?*" the teacher laughed condescendingly, shaking her pencil earrings that someone (probably her cat-sitter or mom) gave her so she could be "the fun professor."

Baron realized how utterly BULLCRAP it was that he sat down just because a teacher told him to—even/especially a fish monster teacher—and that he must've been programmed from an early age to do whatever a bunch of idiots said as long as they were older than him and in an ostensible position of power.

But he wasn't having it anymore.

He summoned all of the nano pump bots swimming around in his bloodstream and inputted cheat codes to make them rewire the crap out of his brain.

Suddenly, he was filled with so much pump that the classroom began to spin. He ripped off his shirt and threw a dozen stink-bomb peg-winders directly at the teacher. They shattered all over her, slicing apart her scales, eyes, and fish lips and mixing her blood with whatever chemicals are in stink bombs.

"*Faaaaaaaart!*" the teacher screamed, either as a general exclamation or because that's what she now smelled like.

The class shrieked and ran for the door.

When they opened it, their screams combined with all the other screams in the hall to create stereo screams, which got Baron even more pumped.

He activated his jet boots and barrel-roll rocketed into the crowd to search for Leila.

But she was nowhere to be found.

22

"Oh, wait, she's right there," Baron said as he spotted her running away with the werewolf vape monster.

Baron blazed over the crowd and grabbed Leila around the waist, scooping her into the air.

As she left the ground, she felt scared—but also intrigued. She didn't know who this stink bomb bad boy was, or where he was taking her, but looking into his manic eyes told her that wherever the destination, it would be intense.

She began to relax and go along for the ride, when suddenly the werewolf vape monster broke her spell.

"Leila!" he vaped. "That's him! That's who killed Count Booswá! That's the perv cop poser!"

"Oh, fucking narc ass," Baron said disgustedly. He lowered a jet boot and maxed out a thruster, torching a hole through the werewolf's chest and releasing a plume of hot grandma egg fart vapor that blasted Baron and Leila out the front door of the school.

The two kept flying until all of the monster students, professors, and cafeteria workers (including a bunch of obese chef monsters) below them transformed into neon marshes and silence.

Well, almost silence.

Leila bit and shrieked through the entire flight.

Baron knew he needed to get her somewhere chill/secluded so he could calmly explain that he *wasn't* a perv cop poser and he only wanted her to bring his best friend back to life.

In the distance, he spotted a giant mountain with foliage in the shape of sideburns. He decided it was as good a place as any.

As soon as he flew over and set Leila down on the mountain's peak, though, she insta-booked it.

"Yo, wait!" Baron called after her. "I just need your help! I don't want to do anything gross to you. I mean, I do, but not if you're not down."

Baron wasn't great at talking to people (or monsters), and ordinarily this would've been when Garindax reminded him to chill. But Garindax was dead, which was the whole point of this thing.

So, Baron chased after Leila while screaming about how he definitely wasn't going to rape her.

She bailed down the mountain, tearing frantically in and out of the sideburnesque vegetation. Baron did his best to keep up, but when he finally reached a clearing, she was gone.

He was just about to give up and dedicate his life to monkhood when he heard her scream, "Perv, help!"

Baron blazed after the voice, wondering if she was talking *about* him, like, "There's a perv after me, so someone help!" or calling *to* him, like, "Yo, Perv (because that's all I know you as, and 'Perv' is faster to say than 'Perv Cop Poser,' and 'PCP' may be too confusing because of the drug), help!"

When he spotted her, he was pumped to see that it was more the latter, but bummed to see a giant rat monster dragging Leila down a black hole in the side of the mountain.

23

Baron raced after Leila and the rat monster, following them into the abyss.

Once inside, he found himself in a labyrinth of dark passages. Beady, red rat eyes glowed in every alcove, and Baron knew he was f-bombed.

The rats crawled out of their hiding places and surrounded him. They all wore sweet punk clothes, like leather jackets and jean vests covered in rat-related patches about spicy cheese or mousetraps or whatever.

One of the rats, probably the leader because he was 7' tall when the rest were closer to 5', pushed his way into the circle.

He rocked a massive beer gut, massiver mohawk, and shades so black the lenses showed you alternate dimensions if you stared into them.

Baron stared, and saw himself reflected as a chubby weakling. He was playing video games by himself in a white-walled, white-carpeted room; his belly covered in cookie crumbs and teardrop stains. He wished the vision was fictitious, but it was factitious—er, factual. Factitious apparently means something different.

But what Baron saw in the shades had actually happened. They were the Dark Days before he started lifting, and before he found Garindax. He had almost forgotten the Dark Days, but now they were right in front of him.

With a mirrored version right in front of the rat monster.

"Well, well, well, what've we got here, boys?" the rodent guffawed, his rat-teeth grill clinking with each laugh. "A little fucking nerd game baby? You lost, little fucking nerd game baby?"

Baron shook his head to clear the image, but he remained frazzled and at minimal pump.

"Dude, where's the babe?" he demanded as toughly as possible.

"What you know about babes, li'l baby?" the rat laughed. The rest of the rats laughed, and their slightly cheaper grills caused a metal cacophony to echo through the cave.

"A lot," Baron snapped. "What do *you* know about babes, *big* baby?"

"Ha! That the best you got?" the rat snorted. "Shit, man, get you some coffee. That shit's *weak*. You phoning it in! Like, whoever controlling yo' verbiage hit the wall. Relyin' on some crutch ass shit. Honky ass shit."

"Oh, uh, well," Baron struggled.

"But allow me to introduce myself. Cho' rude ass coming in here asking about *babes* without even so much as a *hello* first. Mhm. The name is DeShawn Bitches, AKA 'King Rat.'"

"King Rat! King Rat! King Rat!" roared all of the other rats, except for one who looked kind of fucked up. He shouted, "Ring Cat."

"You here in *my* kingdom of Sideburn Mountain," King Rat said as he waved a scaly, bejeweled paw around. "And there ain't no nerd games here, lil' nerd game baby, so I'm thinkin' you must be lost."

"I'm NOT a nerd game baby!" Baron growled, swinging Garindax's pieces over his shoulder and into his hands. "Not anymore. The name is Baron. Baron…von Babegetter, AKA 'King Rip.'"

He made up the last bit since he felt like he needed some extra credibility—especially while holding a broken guitar, surrounded by rat monsters, and when Leila might be in earshot.

It didn't work.

"*Ho, ho!*" King Rat chuckled. "Well, *Baby von Bedwetter*, you about to be 'King R.I.P.'"

24

The rats exploded in laughter and began high-fiving, slapping tails, and pretending to hold each other back.

"You set that right on the tee for me," King Rat wheezed. "I said, '*Wop!* There that ball go.'"

All the rats narrowed their eyes and nodded in deep thought.

Baron had no idea what was going on.

"See, you gotta be quick," King Rat preached. "That's Rule Number One of getting babes. Rule Number Zero is you don't go around sayin' shit like, 'My name is King Rip.'

"*Hi! My name is King Rip*," King Rat mimicked using his white-breadiest voice. "*How are you on this fine day, ma'am? Would you like to buy a vacuum cleaner?*"

The rat monsters figuratively lost their shit. The kind-of-fucked-up one, literally.

King Rat continued, "Now, that's you. And babes don't go in for that shit. Babes don't go in for broke-ass du's holding broke-ass guitars. But those the only freebies you gonna get. You wanna know more, you gotta buy my book: *DeShawn Bitches' Guide to Getting Bitches.* That why you here? You here to buy my book?"

"No," Baron snapped. "I already told you. I know how to get babes. I'm awesome at it. And I'm here to get the one you kidnapped."

"Oh, hell no," King Rat said under breath. "That man say…*mhm.* Audacious. Ostentatious. Nah, man. She mine now. Chapter 9 of *DSBGtGB*, verse 11: If you can't woo 'em, kidnap 'em. Put 'em in the trunk. They always come around."

King Rat winked, and his shades showed Leila chained to a throne made of cheese and tinfoil.

"Heh heh. See?" King Rat sneered. "She like it, she like it." A strand of drool fell from his grilled snout.

Baron became pissed, and then doubly pissed. The fact that he now cared about some chick—on top of all the other bullcrap going on in his life—was too much to handle. Even with the odds and rat monsters stacked against him, he took his shot.

He swung Garindax's body/neck in the air like nunchakus and charged.

"Ha!" King Rat chortled. "This boy think he a samowai!"

He lifted his tree-trunk-sized tail into his paws and prepared to swat the incoming Baron like a gleaming white wiffle ball.

25

King Rat swung his tail at Baron, who used Garindax's body as a skateboard deck to 1080 handbeezy over the incoming appendage. He flipped Garindax's neck around the tail as he launched over it, ensnaring it 500x with a razor-wire low E string.

As Baron landed, and with a swift yank, King Rat's tail flew into the air. A shower of blood and scales followed, spraying across the cave walls and painting them a kind-of semi-gloss, kind-of eggshell magenta. It was nice.

King Rat threw back his head in an agonized shriek, launching his shades off his eyes and onto Baron's. Baron hyperfocused through the multidimensions and saw King Rat for what he truly was—*not a getter of bitches, but a bitch himself.*

Reflected in the shades was a younger, fatter, non-mohawked King Rat. He awkwardly knelt on the edge of a bed, and in his crotch area was a limp/microscopic peener.

A hot slug chick (who looked like a younger, slimier, more-mandarin-less-tangerine version of the waitress from Scrape the Goodie Off) lay naked in front of King Rat. Her nipples were as flat as pancakes, indicating that she wasn't even half turned on.

"No!" screamed the current version of King Rat, who was more concerned about losing his bravado than his tail.

The rat crew turned slowly from the shaded Baron to the shadeless King Rat.

"Stop looking at me!" King Rat cried.

"Stop looking at me!" Young King Rat echoed in the shade-vision. His voice sounded identical to one he had used to mock Baron. "You're making me nervous! And that makes *it* nervous!"

Slug Jugs sighed a super unimpressed sigh. "So, what, I'm supposed to have sex with you with my eyes closed?"

"Yeah," Young King Rat replied hopefully. "You can pretend you're sleeping, and I'm just a ghost or something that comes in and does my thing. That way there'll be no pressure on me, and it'll be like a sexy fantasy for you."

"That's no fantasy," Slug Jugs chided. "I don't fuck around with ghosts. Not anymore. Ectoplasm and shit all over my eyestalks."

She slimed her way upright on the bed and pulled on her shirt. "I also don't fuck around with babies. And, right now, that's you."

"No, wait!" Young King Rat shouted.

He pointed to his wiener, which had grown slightly but remained microscopic. "It's working! Call me a baby again! I'm just a little diaper baby, right?"

"Ugh," Slug Jugs grunted as she slimed off the bed and made her way to the door of King Rats' parents' basement. "You need some self-esteem, Deshondrias. And career aspirations beyond the walls of PetWorld. And deodorant that doesn't have a dragon on the label."

"Oh, *yeah?*" Young King Rat called after her. He fell off the bed and dragged himself across the floor, tugging his taffy rodent dick as he crawled. "Well, you're just a...bitch."

Young Slug Jugs spun around on her slime axis, ready to slap the shit out of Young King Rat with an eyestalk. Instead, she shook her head and turned back to the door.

"You and I both know who the bitch is, Deshondrias."

The door closed, and Young King Rat found himself staring at his reflection in the mirror on the other side, his wiener so non-bonered it was fully concave.

The shade-vision faded out, and everyone turned their attention to Modern King Rat. They no longer saw the mohawk, tattoos, or grill. They saw a tailless wiener child, writhing in a pool of his own blood while still trying to flex his arms to look tough.

"Take me to the ba—Leila," Baron growled. He took off the shades and threw them at the pathetic pile of mess. "*Deshondrias.*"

King Rat scrambled for the shades.

"Ha, now you fucked up!" he cried as he slammed them back onto his beady eyes.

He stared intently at Baron, hoping to see another vision of weakness.

Instead, he saw Baron screaming in a galaxy of blacklight lightning bolts, doing one-armed pullups while shredding on Garindax with the other arm. Bikini babes clamored around him, clawing at his crotch and begging to be taken to the Bone Zone.

King Rat died instantly.

Baron turned to the rat crew. "Um, someone else take me to Leila?"

26

The rat crew led Baron down a series of dark passages packed with pimento cheese and sideburn trimmings.

They eventually reached a small grotto where, in the middle of the floor, Leila was chained.

Her eyes initially lit up at the sight of Baron because she recognized him and he *wasn't* King Rat, but they narrowed when she remembered he was the one who had kidnapped her in the first place.

"Yo, chill," Baron said before she could scream at him. "I'm here to rescue you."

"Yeah, right!" she screamed at him. "You're here to *re-kidnap* me. I was warned about you. You're some kind of perv cop poser."

"Yep. The fucking vapewolf and pencil-peened vampire were right. I'm a perv cop poser. Which leaves you two choices: would you rather chill with a perv cop poser who wears rocket boots and is drenched in cologne, or with a dumpy rat monster named Deshondrias who works at PetWorld?"

Leila looked around the room. Fabric anime posters and empty milk jugs with straws in them were frigg'n *everywhere.*

"Get me the fuck out of here NOW," she said as sternly as a mom on shore leave, whatever that means.

Baron unchained Leila, and the two walked back into the main cave chamber to find the rat crew eating the corpse of their ex-leader because they didn't understand all the thoughts/feelings coursing through their little rodent brains.

Leila shooed them away and looked down at King Rat's remains.

Rage filled her eyes.

She turned to Baron and muttered, "You might want to get out of here unless you want to see some crazy crap."

Baron bailed, and that was the end of his and Garindax's adventure.

THE END

27

JKJKJK.

Baron was always down to see some crazy crap, so he immediately replied, "I'm Pete and Pete."

"Huh?" Leila sputtered.

"Oh, yeah," Baron said. He forgot that when you meet someone new, you have to introduce them to all your bullcrap before just saying it.

"That means 'I'm P and P,'" he explained, "which is short for 'I'm pumped and primed.'"

"How is that *short?*" Leila balked. "It's the same number of syllables. You've just doubly convoluted it."

"Uh, I dunno. I mean, it's definitely faster to say 'P' than 'pumped.'"

Baron alternated saying both a few times to demonstrate. Seeing that Leila wasn't fully sold, he took out his phone and opened a stopwatch app to prove his point.

Leila stopped him.

"But you're not even *saying* 'P.' You're saying 'Pete,' which because of the hard vowel sound takes just as much time to say—if not MORE—as 'pumped.'"

"No way. Pumped is like 'pumped-uh.' It's closer to two syllables."

"This whole fucking thing has gone off the rails," Leila snapped. "Do you want to see some crazy crap, or not?"

"Yes-uh," Baron overarticulated. "I'm pumped-uh and primed-uh."

Leila sighed and knelt next to King Rat's corpse. He looked like he was already starting to rot/bloat, but he actually looked that way before he died.

Leila reached into her bra and pulled out a small velvet pouch. Baron got Pete and Pete because she touched some boob.

She opened the pouch and removed glass vials containing stink blasta-blastas, the proboscis of a tropical PP sucker, lemon zest, and a whisper of cinnamon. She smashed them all together in a mortar, covered her nose/mouth, and sprinkled the mixture over King Rat.

Baron cracked up since he thought she was simply putting gross stuff on him as a final bust. He stopped laughing, though, when she began a spooky chant:

Boo swah somma!
Let's get crazy tonight!
Boo swah somma!
Because the time is so right!

King Rat's body stirred.

"Oh, fuck!" Baron yelled, jumping back.

King Rat sat up. His milky eyes scanned the room until they landed on Leila.

"*Ba-babe?*" he gargled.

"Yes, my king," Leila replied sessily.

"You brought me back…because you love me?"

"No, my king," Leila said less sessily, more pissedly.

"Because you love…*deez?*" He curled a clawed finger and made a repetitive pointing motion at his rocket-launcher rat balls.

Leila smiled and moved toward him, walking super hot/feminine like Jessica Rabbit or Peggy Bundy.

King Rat insta-got pink thing. It looked fucking disgusting, like a gross alien lipstick, and the entire room started to smell like Buffalo Flavor-Blasted Goldfinch Crackers.

"Close," Leila said as she choked back vomit and drew closer to King Rat. "I brought you back to do *this*."

She screamed a crazy mom-scream and stomped the fuck out of King Rat's nuts with her 13" heels.

"*FUUUUEEEEEEEK!*" King Rat shrieked as his balls imploded. His pink thing desiccated into dust, and he died for the second time in like five minutes.

Leila turned to Baron. "Now you know not to fuck with me," she said with a confident smile.

"Totally," Baron said. "Not that I had planned to, but thanks for assuming that about me. Anyway, can we get outta here before inhaling this dude's wiener dust kills us?"

28

Baron and Leila bailed out of the rat cave and back onto Sideburn Mountain's main trail.

"So," she started, beginning to realize that Baron was an okay dude with an okay 'tude. "You want to tell me why you kidnapped me?"

"Oh, yeah!" Baron replied. "I need you to resurrect my best homie, Garindax, so we can get back to this kid's birthday party on Urth."

"Hmm. I don't know what most of those words mean, but I can definitely try. Where are his remains, and how old are they? I may not be able to do anything if he's already rotted. Or even if I could…you may not want me to."

"Why?" Baron asked with a manic grin. "Because sometimes dead is better?"

"Huh? No, because in an advanced state of putrefaction, your 'best homie' may no longer have the connective tissue to stand, the brain matter to think, the eyes to see—"

"Right, right. So, *sometayhms, dead is bettah?*"

"I guess. Is that from a movie or something?"

Baron's heart sank. "Forget it. He's right here."

He swung Garindax's pieces over his shoulder and lovingly reconnected them.

"I don't know exactly how long he's been dead," he said solemnly. "Since before I kidnapped—er, rescued—you. Couple hours, maybe. Days?"

Leila looked down at the guitar pieces and then up at Baron.

He seemed so pained/confused, like a werecat who had jumped into a storm drain and then had no frigg'n clue how to get out.

Baron's sudden vulnerability, coupled with the fact that an instrument was his best friend and he was trying to get back to a kid's birthday party, tugged at Leila's heartstrings like crazy. Even if his face wasn't all that symmetrical and his haircut was kind of shitty, she was starting to dig him.

"Okay," she said gently while lowering her guard for what felt like the first time in years. "Let me see what I can do."

She carefully laid Garindax's reconnected pieces on the trail, knelt by his side, and pulled out her velvet boob pouch (which Baron didn't even think about this time because there was more important stuff at hand).

Leila combined energy drink powder, energy drink liquid, and energy drink slime in her mortar. Then she incanted as she drizzled the pump panacea onto Garindax:

Somma nay shee, somma nay shee!
Hey, everybody, let's get crazy!
Somma nay shee, somma nay shee!
Hey, let's get crazy tonight, baby!

Baron held his breath and waited.

Garindax didn't move.

29

Garindax didn't move—he glowed.

His frets glowed faintly at first, like a bunch of drunk fireflies, but gradually increased in intensity, like a bunch of caffeinated fireflies.

"Oh, *FART YEAH!*" Baron screamed.

Garindax's spider eyes shot open, and in perfect harmony all eight baller-beyond-belief-fact-or-fiction blacklights turned to Baron and winked.

Baron slowly walked over to his best friend in the universe.

As soon as he picked up Garindax, he felt both of their power/pump explode. The two began to hover in midair even though Baron was barely using his rocket boots.

"Hey!" Leila called.

Baron snapped out of his awesome trance and looked down at her.

"Where do you think you're going, *mister?*" she asked playfully.

She smiled and reached for Baron's hand, ready to join him in his pumped air-dance. Ready to join him in his life.

"I told you," Baron said matter-of-factly. "We gotta get to this kid's party."

"But what about our relationship?" Leila pleaded.

"Huh?" Baron asked, still floating higher.

"What about our *relationship?!*" she repeated, her face and voice snapping back into crabby mom mode.

"Fuck that! *Repo Man!* The other one was *Pet Sematary!*"

Baron blasted off into the stratosphere while playing a surf song so insanely sweet that Leila didn't even care about being left heartbroken and alone in the middle of Sideburn Mountain, where she would most likely be devoured by blood vultures or hermit crabs or something.

Probably.

She probably didn't care.

It was fine.

30

Baron and Garindax flew back to the heart of Monsteropolis, doing sweet barrel rolls and flips the entire time.

Upon getting there, the duo noticed that it had become crazy late at night: the sky was ultra black, there were barely any monsters in the streets, and smooth jazz was playing everywhere.

As much as Baron wanted—*needed*—to get back to Little Billy's party, he suddenly realized how long he'd been awake and how tired he was. Even though Garindax wasn't tired because he got to be dead for a while, Baron had to crash if he wanted to be in prime party form.

He couldn't tell which one of the dark buildings surrounding him was a hotel, so he landed over by a phone booth with eyeballs and fangs, busted in, and picked up the receiver.

"'Ello, Monster Telephone Service!" a British-sounding voice crackled over the line.

Fucking EVERYTHING here is "monster," Baron thought. It was getting tedious.

"Yo, operator—" he started.

"Monster operator, yes!" the voice interrupted.

Baron felt nauseated.

"I need a cab."

"A *wot?*"

"A…monster cab," Baron said, dying a little bit inside, "to take me to a…monster hotel."

"Yes, sir! One monster cab monstering to your monster!"

The line clicked off.

Baron exited the phone booth and sat on the curb, hoping that whatever the fuck the operator meant equated to a cab taking him somewhere to crash. He didn't have the pump/patience to deal with any more bullcrap.

As he started to ask Garindax what it was like being dead, since that seemed like something you should ask someone, a gang of dark figures approached.

You fucking guessed it.

They were monsters.

31

The gang's frontman wore a derby hat on his melty slime head and a boogery mustache on his melty slime face. One of the ossified boogs had imprisoned a mosquito that probably could've been used to clone some extinct shit.

Baron didn't know whether he was dealing with a slime monster or a booger monster, but either way he wasn't feeling it.

"Good evening to you, dark sir," the monster said with a bow.

"Bish, keep moving," Baron snapped.

"Oh, but I am offended!" the monster gasped. "Here I am, a humble salesman, approaching you with the sole intent to offer an innocuous—dare I say *most gracious*—business proposition, yet you malign me!"

"Another fucking fancy monster, too. What's with this place?" Baron grumbled. "Look, I barely understand what the fart you're talking about, but whatever you're selling, I ain't buying. We're just waiting for our monster cab."

"Are you so cocksure?"

"Nah, man, we dig boobs."

"No, are you so certain that you *'ain't'* purchasing my wares?"

The monster opened his trench coat, and what looked like a million glowsticks lit up the wet street. Each one had a needle sticking out of it.

"You see," he continued, "I have something for everyone, even the most *uncouth* of patrons."

"Now I'm a hundo thousand bojojillion percent sure, Maury. We don't do drugs. So fuck off."

"My dark sir, you are doubly—nay, triply—mistaken. You *will* do drugs, it is *you* who off shall be fucking, and my name is not '*Maury*.' It is Mephistopheles Stickynails, Esquire. And these are my fine fiends."

The four monsters flanking Mephisto stepped forward as he proprietously introduced them.

"Ragnarok Goldstein, Esq., a being whose polish is as refined as his breeding!"

A fat rock monster wearing an expensive suit crossed his arms and turned up his nose at Baron.

"Trinormous Rex, Esq., financial advisor by day and trade, sommelier by night and passion."

An ice dinosaur coolly bowed.

"Totem Boneapart, M.D., Esq., top of his class at Monster University—the original Sideburn Mountain campus, of course. Four percent acceptance rate."

A tiki monster with a bitchy little face extended a hand.

Baron left him hanging.

"And last, but most assuredly not least, is the mononymous Broome, with his eponymous broom."

A dumpy, pasty, middle-aged humanoid with wispy hair and ped glasses shambled directly over to Baron. He carried in his fish-belly-colored right hand a broom with bristles saturated in blood.

"*Hello there, young man!*" Broome squawked in a high-pitched, warbled voice.

Baron saw a tiny balloon flapping at the back of Broome's throat, and it insta-covered him in goosebumps.

"Back off, ped!" he yelled, pissed that the weirdo had invaded his personal space. He whipped out Garindax and wailed a couple of quick-attack power chords.

Electric wasp stingers materialized from Garindax's fangs and slammed into Broome's chest.

The monster merely smiled and nipped through his dingy button-down shirt.

"Heh heh," Mephisto chuckled. "Simple fool. Your guitar will have no effect on him."

"Why not?" Baron asked. "Is he some kind of deaf ice cream truck driver or something?"

"What? No," Mephisto scoffed. "What a bizarre thing to say. Nay, Broome, like each of his most distinguished forebearers, is a *rap monster*."

"Oh, fuck!" Baron yelled as Broome twisted off the top of his broomstick to reveal a mic with a professional-grade, skull-shaped pop filter.

32

With a twisted grin, Broome began his rap:

Yo, I'm da Broomstah!
*Comin' down hard like *BOOM*stah!*

A sonic wave exploded out of Broome's broomicrophone, sending Baron and Garindax flying backward through the monster phone booth. The receiver fell off the hook and the monster operator yelled, "Oi, there it is! Right in the bollocks!"

As soon as Baron pulled himself to his feet, Broome continued the lyrical barrage:

Break dem boys off
*And I'm platinum like *DOOM*stah!*

Broome's body became encased in platinum. With his non-mic hand, he fanned himself with all five installation floppy disks of Doom II, and his eyes became covered in cacodemon contact lenses. His defense points increased by 4,332.

Y'all know I be doing it half-naked all night!
Do infinity pushups while I crush the mic!

Broome's dingy shirt dissolved to reveal a bunch of sick tribal/corporate sponsorship tattoos while Baron started doing pushups against his will. His pump got a +5, but his endurance a -6, so it definitely wasn't worth it.

B-R-O-to-the-O-M-E!
Cha' boy Broome packing heat
And soon you'll see
That I'm the king!

A black skeleton crown from when BK had a Halloween burger appeared on Broome's head. Baron's awe went up by 29 points, which negatively affected all spellcasting abilities he didn't even know he had.

Pimp from day one!

Platinum Broome became magically becaped, and a pimp cane whooshed into his non-mic hand (he dropped or did something with the Doom II floppy disks—just chill).

The cane was jet black, with a grip the shape of an elephant head on top and a rusty nail on the bottom.

Baron imagined how sweet it would be to tear up anthills with it, and he was instantly filled with jealousy. His boner mana fell, big time.

Step to me punk, and I'll show you my gun!

A tiny derringer appeared in Broome's non-cane hand (the one that was holding the broomic—the fact that he juggled everything made it all the more intimidating).

'Cuz I'm that big, bad Broome
And I inhaled a balloon!
Now I break dem boys off
'Cuz I'm crazy as a loon!

Broome's jaw turned into a bird beak and split down the middle, causing the balloon to flap around like crazy.

Baron had already seen it, though, so it actually didn't have any effect. Plus, the repetitive "break dem boys off" and cliché "crazy as a loon" lines were pretty weak.

He felt an iota of pump/determination. But it wasn't enough, and Broome was fucking relentless.

I be spitting fire like all damn day!
Step to me, punk
And it's you I'm gon' SLAY!

Broome, the mic, the cane, fucking *everything* immediately ignited.

"Oh, how I love a good conflagration," Mephisto swooned. He raised a knee, brought back his foot, and jammed an index finger into the resulting crease before thrusting to the beat of "Jingle Bells" like an absolute maniac.

Broome began levitating and barrel-rolling wildly toward Baron, shooting flames all over the place.

"Dude, book it!" Garindax shouted.

Baron was about to jump out of the way when his ADHD kicked in.

All he could think about was how the Broome missile reminded him of M. Bison's Psycho Crusher attack, and how M. Bison's name came from Mike Tyson; so, in reality, M. Bison was supposed to be Balrog; but Balrog wasn't supposed to be M. Bison, but Vega; and Vega—

Broome slammed into Baron, knocking him out cold and silencing all the bullcrap screaming in his brain.

33

Baron awoke to find himself covered in glass/cuts.

He and Garindax had been launched all the way across the street and through the window of an ancient pharmacy.

On the pump side, they had landed in a display of glow-in-the-dark rubber mummies. On the anti-pump side, Mephisto and his gang were now standing over them.

Each member held a neon syringe.

"So cocksure..." Mephisto said as he leaned down to inject the drugs into Baron's ears and Garindax's spider ears.

Suddenly, an egg-shaped monster cab blazed up and slammed into the drug dealer, splattering his slime/booger body across the windshield.

"*Fucking little street traaaaa...*" Mephisto oozed before the cab's windshield wipers wiped him from existence.

The surviving gang members shot back in horror, giving Baron enough room to swing Garindax across his body and into all of their syringes.

The syringes shattered, and the liquid content sprayed onto the monsters and was instantly absorbed into their faces and/or pee holes via pants osmosis.

"*NOOOO!*" they cried as their pupils exploded and the drugs took effect:

Totem saw the world as if someone had turned on a "Big Head Mode" cheat, which are *always* stupid and a great way to vet new buddies. If they want to turn that crap on while you're playing *NBA Jam* or something, you need to nip that shit "in the butt."

It *kind of* makes sense for *Goldeneye* or *Turok* where you can go for headshots, but even then it's not worth it because you have to deal with goon laughter all night—or at least until your friend notices your VHS copy of *Cannibal Holocaust* and calls his mom to come pick him up because he thinks you're a "demon," which he says like "diamond" because he's from some small town in West Virginia. Fuck Big Head Mode.

Anyway, Totem felt the pain on an intensely ironic level. He took out his pouch of head-shrinking powder and imagined sprinkling the precise dose needed to make everything around him normal-sized again. But since he was on drugs, he actually just snorted the crap out of it while pissing himself and screaming in a progressively higher pitch until his head popped like a tiki teen pimple.

Trinormous Rex groaned and grabbed his stomach. The drugs had caused radical chemical changes in the gallons of wine sloshing around in the sommelier's guts. Malbec became Blueberry Blitz Mad Dog; chardonnay turned to Límónád 7 Loco; and petite sirah spoiled into one of these "hard sodas" that are simply malt beverages like the others, only given a fancy label and marked up 500%.

The concoction bubbled so violently that it burned a hole through his ice body and spilled onto the street. Trinormous Rex let out a groan, wavered, and crashed against the asphalt, shattering into a high-ABV jigsaw puzzle.

Ragnarok had an existential crisis and called an ex-girlfriend from high school. Within a year, they were married and had too many kids with too many *y*'s in their names.

Only Broome stood standing standingly.

He smiled at Baron and said, "*Miiiild*. Thanks for the free hit—now it's your turn!"

34

Baron and Garindax were floored.

Broome had absorbed an entire syringe of monster drugs and barely even felt it. And what he had felt, he dug.

The duo realized fearfully that they were facing a monster who knew not only how to rap, but how to *party*.

Broome raised his broomic and shambled forward. He opened his mouth, ready to unleash another onslaught of rhymes. The balloon at the back of his throat inflated.

Baron prepared himself to die/fry eggs for the first time; Garindax, for the second.

As the rap monster rapped his first word, an electric *SCHOOM!* silenced it.

Broome's ped glasses clattered to the ground, and the balloon flopped around in his neck cavity amidst a shower of blood and neon monster drugs. As it deflated, the hideous stench of crawl spaces wafted across the air.

Finally, Broome's body toppled over and revealed a mysterious figure standing in the shadows.

The dark shape busted a ridiculously intense power stance, and Baron suddenly found himself staring down the barrel of a Buttons-9000 Pulse Rifle.

35

Behind the rifle and plume of haunted house fog that shoots out whenever a B9000-PR is fired, a glow-in-the-dark beak smirked.

A stoic bird monster walked over and extended a feather. Baron grabbed it and pulled himself off the ground.

"You sliced and diced," the bird said.

"Thanks, man. You, too," Baron responded.

"No. You cut. From glass."

Baron looked down and noticed that he was bleeding all over the place.

"Oh, crap," he muttered.

The bird reached into his utility belt and pulled out a flask of neon liquid. He held it out to Baron.

"Here," he said. "Drink."

"Yo, I know you missed it," Baron said exasperatedly, "but I just went into a whole thing about how we don't do drugs. That's why there are all these dead dudes chilling."

"This not drugs. This potion."

The bird monster gave a thumbs-up and winked a hologram eye.

"Oh, right on," Baron said. He grabbed the flask and took a swig.

It was *legit*, like an ice-cold Josta.

"Fart, that's good!" Baron exclaimed as half of his cuts insta-healed and his pump increased eightyfold.

"Can I give it a world?" Garindax asked.

He was still in the pharmacy's window display.

The fact that Baron had forgotten about him, coupled with the pitifulness of Garindax saying "give it a world," made him feel super guilty.

"Definitely, homie," he replied while slinging his buddy back across his chest.

Even though it meant the other half of his cuts may not heal, Baron poured the rest of the potion into Garindax's output (food/drink input) jack.

"Dude, this rules!" Garindax yelled in perfect tune. "Tastes sorta like Josta."

The mutual sentiment made Baron even more confident in his decision to share. Plus, he might get some sweet scars out of the non-healed cuts, so it was win-win.

As the potion took effect, Garindax's fangs/strings became crazy sharp/polished, and his eyes glowed brighter than when he was a spiderling lute.

"Too rude," the bird said in a pleased tone. "P.S., I Nerp X. You call monster cab?"

"Hell yeah!" Baron and Garindax shouted. They rushed over to the cab, slammed into the backseat, and didn't buckle up.

The interior of the cab looked amazing, with eggplant-purple pleather seats and a fluorescent orange soft-top made of spiderwebs. Up front hung a pair of anthropomorphic monster dice, which growled and bit each other like pumped wolf brothers.

Nerp X jumped through the open window into the driver seat and turned his glow-beak to his new passengers/best friends.

"Where go?"

"Closest monster hotel, I guess," Baron replied. He wasn't even all that tired anymore, but he knew that he and Garindax needed to crash for a while since neither of them got a full potion heal.

"Ka," Nerp X cawed.

He flipped one switch to turn on the meter, and then another to turn on the black metal. All the lyrics were about bird stuff, only darker: intentionally flying into windows, regurgitating chewed-up baby birds into the mouths of giant worms, mite parasitism, brood parasitism, etc.

The monster cab jammed through the empty streets, blazing by pitch-black buildings and Mountain Dew Pitch Black fountains. They repeated like a wraparound background in a cheap cartoon.

It was hypnotic.

Then, soporific.

Baron's eyes shot open as he heard tires screech and Nerp X scream, "*Fuuuuuuuuuuck!*"

36

"What the crap!" Baron shouted as he awoke with a start. "What happened?!"

"We here," Nerp X replied. "So I pumped."

"Oh, man, nothin' wrong with that!" Baron said, getting a sweet contact pump going.

He kicked open the cab door, grabbed Garindax, and threw a wad of Urth money and birdseed into the passenger seat in case Nerp X was down for one but not the other.

"*Fuuuuuuuuuuck!*" the bird monster yelled while chucking both into his glow beak.

He tore off into the night, weaving across both lanes of traffic. In the dense Monsteropolis fog, his tail lights wrote in perfect cursive, *This city here is like an open sewer; you should just flush it right down the fuckin' toilet.*

"Taxi drivers," Baron laughed.

He turned to face the monster hotel and was met with the snarling snout of a gigantic, tusked rhinocerbellhop.

"*BAGS?*" it golem-groaned while searching around Baron's feet.

"Nah, man," Baron answered. "You can chill. We don't have any." He tried circumnavigating the monster, but it stepped in front of him and furrowed its brow.

"*BAGS!*" it growled, raising a door-sized hand to stop the duo from proceeding.

"Oh, *BAGS!*" Baron mimicked. "I thought you said, 'brags,' or 'frags,' or 'soft-shell crabs,' or 'do you have the guts to take home a glowing piece of the crag.' But you said, 'bags'?"

"*BAGS,*" the monster confirmed with a nod.

"Gotcha. Well, you're in luck! We definitely have bags. And guess what?"

The rhinocerbellhop leaned in hopefully.

"*SOOO DO YOU!*" Baron shouted in a sweet game show announcer voice. He swung Garindax between the monster's legs, smashing him right in the ding-dong and ding-dong sack.

The monster's eyes/tusks crossed as he grabbed his crotch, fell to the ground, and violently vomited.

He knew that he needed to get to a hospital, fast. His mind raced with thoughts of how he didn't have health insurance, and how he never should've left culinary school and abandoned his dream of becoming an obese chef monster. Those thoughts were quickly replaced with ones about internal bleeding; irreparable reproductive damage; his wife sobbing when he tells her he can't give her a child—she had been asking for years, but "the time just wasn't right," and now it never would be. He began to cry and writhe on the cement.

"Yeah, right in the bean bag!" Garindax laughed.

He and Baron slapped five and busted into the monster hotel.

The lobby looked so baller. It was at least 300 floors high and atrium style, so when Baron looked up he saw every type of monster partying outside its room: eyeball monsters, mom monsters, obese chef monsters, you-name-it (especially if you're feeling more creative).

A steady stream of the guests fell/were pushed over the balcony railings while an equally steady stream of janitor roach monsters swept the carcasses from the lobby into the kitchen.

On the left was an indoor pool filled with swamp water, swampranha, and swampsharks. Bikini babes of all colors, shapes, and scalinesses sat around the pool and took pictures of themselves. Obese, speedoed perv monsters surrounded the babes while also taking pictures and mumbling about popping boners.

To the right of the pool was a tiki bar backed by a toxic octopus monster who slung drinks in every direction. Werewolves, vampires, chainsaw monsters, and Daves chugged then straight-up ate the tiki mugs before another appeared like magic in their hands/paws/whatevers.

The sights got Baron and Garindax pumped in a major way, but they quickly remembered that they came to the hotel to sleep now so they could party later.

They walked over to the check-in desk, where an emaciated frog monster sat with his legs crossed like a lady. He winked, and it made the duo feel weird enough to serve as a cliffhanger.

37

"Welcome to ze Monster Hotel, booswahs," the frog whispered through a dewy mustache. "Do we have a reservation?"

"What the fuck did you call us?" Baron demanded.

"Never you mind, meh petit booswah. It is just French, as are we. Monsieur LeDouche, at your service. Your pleasure. Your *pleasurable service.*"

Baron and Garindax bristled.

"Me and my guitar need a room to crash in for a few hours," Baron said after unbristling.

"Meh guitar and *we,*" LeDouche corrected. "But who are we to judge ze grammar and lifestyle of one who requests ze, mm, *hourly* rate? Going to make some sweet-petit music, are we? *Hmm?*"

He slowly winked his left eye at Baron, and then his right eye at Garindax. Frog eye boogers crusted all over his lapel.

Any other time, Baron would've leapt over the counter, grabbed a bunch of keys off their hooks, and started stabbing until all that remained was a dewy mustache.

But he was too frigg'n tired.

"Exactly," he sighed. "Sweet/petit music, booswahs and all that bullshit. Just give us a room."

"But of course," LeDouche replied with lips now peppered with eye boogers.

He turned his head and spit a ropelike blue tongue at the wall of keys. He then spun back around and flopped his tongue onto the front desk. It looked and smelled like a plastic fishing lure covered in key-shaped fishhooks.

"Take your petit pick," he murmured while wriggling it back and forth.

Baron reached for the nearest, least disgusting key. It was shaped like a skeletal arm with fingers as the bit (the part that goes in the door). On the bow (the part that's held and turned—look up "parts of a key" since this shit isn't intuitive) was written “Room 1331,” a number that’s spooky up front and Halloweeny on the back.

“*Ooo*, but you have tickled meh taste buds!” LeDouche gasped as Baron grabbed the key.

“Exactly,” Baron sighed again. He turned and bailed to the elevators.

A chubby, pallid goblin kid stood there waiting. He held an energy drink in each hand and must’ve come from the pool because he had a damp towel wrapped around his neck and a sopping wet bowl cut on top of his head.

“I already pressed the button,” the goblin kid said to Baron through chattering teeth.

“Uh, cool, man. Good job,” Baron replied.

“You’re welcome,” the kid chattered, even though Baron hadn’t actually said “thanks.”

While they waited for the elevator to arrive, the goblin stared at Baron and shivered; Garindax made an annoying “bing” noise every time the floor indicator light changed; and Monsieur LeDouche waved and yelled, “Bonsoir, baby booswahs!” since he felt like he hadn’t received enough attention.

It was a living hell.

Finally, the elevator car groaned its way down to the lobby.

Baron busted in and pressed the button for Floor 13. The goblin kid followed and pressed each fucking button on the panel, including the alarm.

Every monster in the hotel turned its eyes/eyestalks to the source of the piercing sound.

Half of the mom monsters judgmentally shook their heads, believing Baron was some shitty dad letting his kid "run wild" even though they had no idea where their *own* babies were at the time (probably dead). The other half clutched their monster pearls, worried that if Baron and the goblin kid weren't related, that obviously meant Baron was a ped by coincidental maleness and proximity.

Both momster halves shot looks to each other, did little eyerolls, and mouthed, "*I don't know!*"

They immediately felt vindicated. They had publicly acknowledged that there was an issue and they were aware of it. Whatever happened now was out of their hands, and if an actual problem arose, their husbands could deal with it.

None of the monster dads gave a fuck about who was in the elevator. They were too busy staring into their glasses of barrel-aged slime bourbon, reflecting on their regrets.

The mondads looked wistfully at the piano in the corner. They thought about how they still didn't know how to play an instrument, and how they had enrolled in Guitar I during their freshman year at Monster University before their own mondads told them that music was for "monfags" so they should take Calculus XVII instead. That way, if/when they fucked up as their mondads knew they would, they could try again the next semester and still have a chance of being admitted to MU's prestigious Fuzzbee Stickynails School of Monsternomics. If you weren't in by your sophomore year, you'd be sucking shit and eating rat food the rest of your life.

So, they switched.

With a grimace, the dads took a sip of slime bourbon and promised to themselves that they would never do that to their own monkids.

But they knew they would.

They took another sip.

They wondered if in the future their kids would respect them; they wondered at what point in the past their wives had stopped.

At what point did they have to start asking—*begging*—their wives for sex like a lowly weregoo instead of apologizing that they couldn't go more than three times in one night?

At what point did the cute 20-something vampcat cashiers, whom the monster dads thought couldn't be more than five years younger when it was actually closer to twenty, start calling them "sir" and smiling sympathetically instead of suggestively?

They exhaled and turned their collective gaze from the piano back to their glasses.

By the time they were retired and had the time to learn an instrument, their hands would be too arthritic, their eyes too weak, their brains too foggy, their backs too sore.

Fuck it.

Music was for monfags, anyway.

They raised a fully capable claw and ordered another drink.

Baron swallowed hard, suddenly feeling like he had stepped on someone's toes. Relief came as the elevator door closed and he and Garindax were alone again.

Until a chubby pallid hand tugged at his shirt, and he remembered they weren't alone at all.

38

"Hey," the goblin kid said.

"Hey," Baron replied.

"Syrup," Garindax called from Baron's back.

The kid took a swig from one of his two energy drinks. "This is so good. 'Sa got cherry."

"Cool," Baron nodded. He had no idea what to do with that.

He looked down at the can, which portrayed a shrieking mandrill and the words "Gr-Ape Ape Executioner" beneath it—nothing about cherry, and kind of strange that they would negate their own pun.

The new buddies, now fully talked out, rode the rest of the way in silence. The only sounds came from the kid chugging/burping his energy drink while Garindax continued his "bing" noises as they stopped on every floor.

Still, it was less of a living hell than before.

"Take it easy, dude," Baron told the goblin kid when they finally reached Floor 13.

"Take it easy, Scott Cherry," Garindax echoed.

"'Night," the kid belched. He attempted to drink from both cans at the same time, which instead resulted in him spilling all over the carpeted floor.

Baron walked down the hall to room 1331, slammed in the key bit, and twisted the bow.

He and Garindax cautiously busted into the room, not knowing what to expect from a monster hotel.

It was par for the fucking course.

To their immediate right was a bathroom, where a sickly yellow light flickered and illuminated a dump-covered everything.

The main room in front of them featured a bed with a duvet composed entirely of a writhing mass of bedbugs. An ancient A/C window unit screeched behind it, blowing out dust and bonus bedbugs.

Baron was about to lose all pump and die when he noticed a ratty CRT TV chilling on a stand against the wall. Attached to it was a Monster 64 video game controller.

He rushed over and pressed the TV's power button. A cheesy welcome page glowed onto the screen and showcased the bar's tiki drinks and pool hours. Baron excitedly navigated past the bullshit bill-pay options and monster porn movies until he confirmed that the hotel indeed had video games. There was even another controller tucked away behind the TV, so he and Garindax could play 2P.

"Oh, *HELLLLLLL YEAH!*" Baron shouted. He hadn't seen a setup like this in over a decade, and it was so rad that it made up for everything else shitty about the room, which was everything.

His—and consequently Garindax's—pump levels shot through the asbestos-filled popcorn ceiling, and they insta-forgot how tired they were.

It was time to party.

They called monster room service and ordered a stack of grilled cheeses, a mountain of fries with tiny glass ketchup bottles, and a dozen Gr-Ape Ape Executioners that were delivered in iced glasses with cellophane wrap over the top instead of in cans for some weird hotel reason.

Baron and Garindax ate junk and played rubbish until nights became days.

They laughed about all the bullshit that came before, and they didn't think about any of the bullshit that was to come.

Eventually, they passed out on the floor, with controllers in hand as pause music repeated in the background and an image of two warriors burned its way into the CRT's screen. It was a screen most would've deemed obsolete: past the time when someone should use it to play M64 games—past the time when someone should use it to play games at all.

But the duo slept peacefully in the screen's soft glow, tucked away from such opinions in one of the countless rooms of The Monster Hotel: a lazily-named place inhabited by countless stupid monsters, in a city in a world in a universe inhabited by countless more stupid monsters.

Meanwhile, back at PizzArea 64, Little Billy's party continued simply because it needed to. And because it could.

39

Baron and Garindax slept for a million.

They only awoke when a veevitch housekeeper busted into their room.

"Pardon may!" she sang. "House-kayping! I jus' nayd to feed and milk them bedbugs rayht quick."

Thinking redneck ninjas were busting in to murder him, Baron shot up, grabbed Garindax, and began shredding.

The last thing the housekeeper saw—before a sick speed metal riff solidified into steel and tore through her neck—was Baron's morning wood. Her head rolled into the hall with its eyes and mouth fully open/prepared for piece.

"Oh, dang," Baron said, realizing his impetuousness. "Sorry about that."

"Wake and shank, man," Garindax reassured.

"Doesn't rhyme," Baron snapped.

He felt embarrassed for sleeping too long, and for acting too hastily with what could've been his new girlfriend.

Baron stared at the veevitch's corpse and imagined driving around with it on a sunny summer day. Her head would still be attached, and they'd blaze to Taco Bell before looking for horror VHS at flea markets and Halloween stuff at Party City. She wouldn't really be interested, but she'd feign pump the whole time because she was cool like that, and he'd reciprocate by watching garbage reality TV shows with her that night. They'd both have Texan accents and life would be beautiful.

"Let's get out of this shithole," Baron growled, not wanting to torture himself any longer with thoughts of what might've been.

"You got it, man," Garindax replied. "But, hey, playing nerd games all night rocked, huh?"

Baron looked over at the controllers and room-service trays scattered across the ground. His existential sadness was quickly replaced by nostalgic pump.

"Hell yeah," he laughed. "Hey, remember that shitty beat 'em up? Where all the enemies were palette-swaps and/or super racist, and that one boss was legit unbeatable? Good times."

The two walked out of the room and over the housekeeper's severed head. She wasn't *that* hot, and Baron realized she probably would've given him shit for wanting to go to Party City two days in a row, totally disregarding the fact that Halloween stuff can hit the shelves *any frigg'n day* once it's summer, and even just seeing unopened boxes labeled "Larry Leviathan's Deluxe Dinosaur Dracula Fangs" stacked on the floor was reason enough to check religiously.

"Sorry about snapping at you, homie," Baron apologized.

"No prob, Bobby Babino the Rip King," Garindax replied.

"Totally rhymes."

Shit was getting kind of weird, so the two busted back down to the lobby to check out.

There, they found Monsieur LeDouche still chilling behind the counter with his legs crossed like a lady. He had winked out so many eye boogers since they last saw him that stalagmites had formed on his lapel.

"Checking out, baby booswahs?" he called as they approached.

"Yep," Baron said as he threw the key on the counter. After feeling guilty for beheading the housekeeper, he chose to once again follow the path of least resistance/bloodshed/interaction with MLD.

"How much do we owe in Urth bucks?" he asked. "Five? Ten?"

"Let meh find out," the frog monster replied. He opened a ledger bound in human flesh and written in human blood and pen ink.

"138 hours for ze room, plus room service, petit video games, and housekeeper homicide *EEEEEEZ*...$88 hundo."

"We can't afford that!" Baron yelled. "We only have, like, $.05 hundo."

"*C'est la vie*," the frog monster replied with a wink that caused the stalagmites to grow. "Lucky for you, we have...how do you say...*other* ways to settle zees matters?"

"No fuck' way!" Baron yelled, covering his crotch.

"Oh, meh petit booswah," MLD laughed. "It is not your ping-pong zat we want; it is your immortality! But if you are offering ze combo deal..."

In a frog-green flash, Monsieur LeDouche leapt over the counter holding aloft the Scarab of Mithyngal!

That's bad.

40

Baron front-flip-dodged Monsieur LeDouche's attack before he even had time to consider whether he was actually immortal (he's pretty sure he wasn't).

The frog monster ate it, hard, sliding across the marble floor and into a trash can by the tiki bar.

When he emerged, a banana peel hung off the top of his head like a stupid little wig and everyone at the bar frigg'n lost it. One fat wereowl laughed so hard that slime bourbon came out of his beakstrils, and since it stung a little bit he let it ruin his entire business trip.

LeDouche leapt out of the trash, feeling super pissed/embarrassed, and shrieked a high-pitched French war cry. He again launched himself at Baron, but this time with his tongue *out.*

Baron swiftly laid down a sludgy doom metal riff on Garindax.

The hotel walls began to melt and slough off into sweet puddles, and a bolt of ice lightning shot out of Garindax's spider fangs and blasted into the airborne frog monster.

MLD's body careened past Baron into the wall, shattering into exactly 88 hundo pieces. It looked almost identical to the Sub-Zero scene from the first *Mortal Kombat* movie, but different enough to not be a ripoff.

"Fatal move," Baron said with a chuckle.

He walked over to the ice-chunks to search them for loot/gold. As he dug through the slush, the Scarab of Mithyngal, totally unfrozen, flew out like a cockroach that doesn't reveal its flying ability until it's too fucking late.

Baron knew he didn't have time to play a single defense note, so he closed his eyes and prepared to die—or at least lose the immortality he may or may not have.

41

"Burp," Garindax burped.

Baron opened his eyes.

The Scarab of Mithyngal was gone.

"Cool, bail?" Garindax asked nonchalantly.

"Dude! Where's that horrifying beetle thing?"

"Oh, I ate it. I'm part spider monster, remember?"

"But what about its fangs? Won't they steal your immortality?"

"Oh, I'm not immortal. I'm part guitar, remember?"

Feeling confident/bored now that everything had settled down, Baron and Garindax busted out of the hotel and back onto the street.

A massive parade was going on, with monsters on both sides of the sidewalk cheering like crazy while floats, clowns, obese chef monsters, and cages of growling retylornynxes tore down the block.

"Oh, fartknockers!" Baron yelled. "Frigg'n monster circus time!"

An obese troll mom standing in front of Baron whirled around. Two stupid, wild-haired troll babies were suckling upon her fat teats. They all had a unique, indescribable smell that the majority of the other monsters hated, but a few loved so much that they created an "I <3 trolldor (troll odor)" subreddit.

"*Excuuuse you?!*" she howled. "You need to watch your fuck' mouth! There are children here!"

Baron had no clue what she was talking about. There was no way she could've been pissed about "fartknockers" or "frigg'n." He thought *maybe* it was because he had said "monster," like it was the "m-word" or something there. But that would've meant they named their city "M-wordopolis," so it couldn't have been that either.

The more confused he felt, the more pissed he became. He also fucking hated when people said "excuse you."

So, he poked the bear.

"What the fartknockers are you talking about, you frigg'n monster circus?" he said as pissed/pumped as possible.

"Why, you white-trash ass..." the troll mom started.

"Time!" Garindax cut in. "You forgot to say 'time.' What the fartknockers are you talking about, you frigg'n monster circus *time?!*"

The troll mom freaked the fuck out. She turned bright purple (she was green before), and both troll babies started crying even though they still had mouths full of nip.

Her eyes went crazy, and she frantically looked around for assistance because she felt slightly victimized/inconvenienced and thus believed everyone should drop whatever they were doing to help with the bullshit minutiae she had going on at the moment. If it was important to her, it should be to everyone else, too.

When she saw that no one gave a crap, she sighed loudly/angrily. When that didn't work, she started crying like her little troll babies.

"This hume assaulted me!" she sobbed.

It was a total lie, but since she hadn't gotten the response she wanted, she needed to turn it up a notch. After exactly two seconds, she even began to believe her lie, which caused her to shake and sob harder.

A few monsters turned around and looked ready to rock.

"He attacked me and my children!" she wailed. "He's a demented pervert! Won't someone do something?!"

More monsters turned around, including a few demented perverts who were hoping to see some shit.

"What?!" Baron demanded. "I didn't do *anything*. I'm sorry if my *words* made you *feel* uncomfortable, but..."

The troll mom cut him off. "Rapist!" she screamed at the top of her lungs. Her poop-butted babies swayed back and forth on her chest, crying and gnawing crabbily.

The monster bystanders cracked their knuckles and moved toward Baron and Garindax.

"Wait, wait, wait," Baron laughed, his bullshit meter going off the charts. "I'm actually *not* sorry. Because guess what? I didn't do crap!"

The mom and encroaching monsters gasped.

"Kill him!" a whiskered blue meanie shouted. "Take his fucking life! I'm sure he deserves it—look at his face! It's kind of asymmetrical! And she's a mom who's just trusting her mom instincts!"

A green botsweenie nodded and gurgled, "Rape him to death with his guitar's razor-wire neck! That'll teach the pervert!"

Both monsters frothed at the mouth and started popping boners.

Baron lost his shit. "Fine! Fuck it! You want me to be a villain?!"

The monsters all widened their eyes hopefully.

"Well, *HEEEERE* you go!" Baron screamed in his maniacal game show announcer voice.

He played a frenetic thrash melody that changed Garindax's fangs to necrotoxic mode. He then swung Garindax into the left troll baby, injecting both fangs into the little jerk at full force/venom.

The baby swung around the nip at light speed while rotting and screaming, "*Mommyyy, heeelllp meeee! Heeeellllp baaaby!*"

Troll milk and blood rained down from the sky, soaking into the dirt and guaranteeing nothing would ever grow there again.

The crowd jumped back, aghast yet fully entertained. The blue meanie crammed his hand into his pocket and went to town.

"*NOOOOO!* My precious Ylyxyndyr!" The troll mom cried as she watched her child reduced to a tan, rotten shell.

Before she could process what had happened, Baron launched a flying, jet-boot-powered knee at the other baby. The tiny jerk rocketed upward but maintained a strong bite on the nip, stretching it 555 feet into the air before turning and starting its descent.

"Don't worry, Baby Ylyxyndry!" the troll shrieked while twisting her belly jewel in a panic. "Mommy will catch you!"

But she missed.

The troll-ling slammed onto the pavement, its fall cushioned only by the rubbery rope of nip dangling from its mouth. Dazed and pleading, it looked to Baron for mercy.

"*THE SLEDGE-O-MATIC!*" he announced instead, his eyes indicating that he had gone totally fucking off the rails. He raised Garindax above his head and brought him down hard.

The monster spawn exploded in a shower of guts and watermelon seeds that sprayed all over the parade-goers who were now cheering in their freshly donned, Baron-branded ponchos.

All they had wanted to see was some violence. They didn't care how they got it or who was on the delivering/receiving end.

Besides, now that the mom's boobs were all chewed up and stretched out, she was less attractive than Baron. That led them to the conclusion that she had been the bad guy all along, and justice had been served. It was a fantastic twist. Everything was fantastic.

"Thank you, thank you!" Baron yelled to his adoring fans. He bowed and shredded an epic speed metal riff on Garindax, who winked his eight eyes at everyone.

The troll mom was dumbfounded. She was always used to getting her way, but this time she hadn't.

Or maybe she had.

After all, she had wanted trouble and attention, and she got both. But now her kids were dead, and her boobs were the grossest in the world.

She closed her eyes and vowed that if she ever had kids again, she'd define herself as something other—something more—than "just a momster." She would find a way to contribute something to monsterkind so she could stop being so defensive out of sheer boredom.

She smiled and opened her eyes, prepared to start anew.

"*ENCORE!*" Baron and Garindax dual game-show announced as the former planted the latter into the ground, raised his jet boots, and blasted off the troll mom's boobs with blacklight flame.

"*Roasted and tuh-tuh-tuh-toasted!*" Garindax shouted over the roaring crowd.

The troll mom gurgled pitifully as her torso disintegrated, revealing the raucous monsters on the other side.

As her body collapsed, two imps rushed over, bent down, and stuck their heads through her open boob cavities. They reared back up, wearing the troll mom's dying body like a tandem hat, and began to dance around and take selfies with their fellow parade-goers.

It was getting a bit too intense.

"Monster circus?" Baron asked Garindax.

"Monster circus," Garindax responded, choking back vom as he watched the troll mom's head flop back and forth—her dead eyes open and staring.

42

Baron and Garindax followed the monster parade until they reached a midway that stretched as far as their ten eyes could see.

It was blacklit as fuck, with commercial haunts and funhouses all over the place. Calliope music played through hidden speakers in the bushes, and a few were slightly out of sync so it sounded extra spooky.

Werewolf barkers called out to passersby, goading them into flipping frogs into vats of acid or throwing darts at newborns.

Vendor carts lined the path and were helmed by obese chef monsters hawking razorblade-filled candied apples, funnel cake made of intestines, and $10 sub sandwiches with only one slice of dry turkey and one leaf of super pale/wilted lettuce.

Baron and Garindax were too broke to do anything, so they kept busting down the midway until they reached a large tent with "Big Top Terror" scrawled above it.

The entrance flap was blocked by a ripped ghost bouncer whose hands were tucked beneath his biceps to make them look even bigger.

"Got tickets/money?" he wailed as Baron and Garindax approached.

The duo walked right through his dumbass and into BTT. They grabbed a seat on the highest bleacher and scooped up some floor popcorn to munch on.

As the lights went down, all of the monsters in the crowd instantly went into coughing fits or yelled "Wooo!" and "Uh oh, I think it's starting!" It made Baron feel closer to them, yet also way more resentful.

A skeleton wearing a top hat and candy-striped jacket busted into the center ring. From the rafters, a mangy rat monster followed him with a spotlight and drooled onto the glass, so a bunch of sweet/gross patterns were projected to the ground below.

"Ladies and gentlemon," the ringleader started. "Your attention, please. Welcome to the *fangulous*, the most *spooptacular* event in monstertainment history! Put your claws together for the *Creppiest Creepers Variety Hour!*"

A group of monsters ran out holding up their arms like dinosaurs.

"Maybe it'll get pumped..." Baron whispered to Garindax—and to himself.

But it *didn't* get pumped.

Instead, the monsters began flailing around and singing like idiots.

"*Meet the monsters! Meet the monsters!*" they sang, shaking their little shoulders back and forth while pretending they had boobs.

Baron and Garindax curled their lips and melted into their seats.

"*We're not your average—*" (an emaciated chicken monster made a stupid little "boo-ba-dee-boop!" noise while doing jazz hands and making his eyes go crazy) "*—ordinary monsters! Meet the monsters! Meet the MOOOONSTERS!*"

Baron and Garindax had seen enough (and didn't want to get sued for copyright infringement). They flagged down a pimply goon vendor, snagged two snowcones, and launched them at the center ring.

Baron's snowcone nailed the chicken monster right in the beak and was immediately followed by Garindax's, which split Baron's clean in two.

The chicken let out a falsetto shriek that silenced the entire tent—except for two dudes, who were cracking up like fucking crazy.

"Oh my fuuuck!" Baron laughed. "Dude, you frigg'n Robin Hooded it!"

"Heh heh, totally!" Garindax laughed.

He had no idea what that meant, but he didn't let on because he didn't want to bring down the pump. But then he worried that if Baron had also "rob-and-hided" his snowcone, like if it just meant to hit someone in the face, then he might be waiting for Garindax to congratulate him, too.

"You did it!" Garindax yelled. But by then three minutes had passed, and he and Baron were being dragged outside by security guard monsters.

43

Baron and Garindax resisted their arrest: the former biting, kicking, and repeatedly asking, "Officer, what did I do? But officer, what did I do?" while the latter slashed at the security guards' arms with razor-wire strings and shouted, "Please, officer, please! Please, officer, please!"

Garindax's method was far more effective, and the security guards were quickly diced into fine chunks.

"Nice! Good job murdering them forever," Baron praised.

"Fucking rob-and-hided 'em!" Garindax said proudly.

"Yeah, I guess. But, yo, let's bust back to the midway and check out some of the dark rides. You know a haunted house *in* Monsteropolis has gotta rock."

As Baron stepped over the security guard remnants, tiny little hands shot out and grabbed his ankles.

"What the fart?" he gasped.

The hands grew bigger, and their grips tighter. Miniature arms grew behind them, then torsos, legs, and peeners/thangs depending on if they were dudes or chicks. Finally, security monster heads wearing security monster hats popped out of each 13' tall, shiny new monster.

"Oh, fucknockers!" Baron screamed. "Dude, they're infini-monsters!"

Garindax ran bioscans and, to his terror, confirmed Baron's suspicion: the security guards were composed of a unique type of Mars mud that had regenerative properties and a pleasant pumpkin scent.

Slicing them into bits would only spawn a new monster from each bit. Frying them into ash would result in a new monster for each, uh, ash. Freezing them would've worked because Baron and Garindax could've booked it before the monsters defrosted, but they weren't able to think of that in time because of the "game show effect."

The game show effect derives its name from the fact that whoever goes on a game show will find it infinitely harder to answer questions, complete pie-based physical challenges, or assemble silver monkeys in that environment—no matter how many seasons they spent screaming at the TV about how much they'd wreck if they got on.

But since Baron and Garindax were *on* the game show instead of chilling in their living room on the pink recliners that they painted to look like go-karts, they were dragged through the streets and thrown into monster jail.

Monster jail was housed in a gigantic limestone castle blanketed in wanted posters.

"Shit, dude. Check," Baron said, noticing that most of the posters depicted crude drawings of him and Garindax. Beneath their sketches, crimes were listed:

–Taking More Than One Candy
–Momstercide
–Destruction of Property/Gatecide
–School Stinkbombing
–Witchnapping
–Veevitchslaughter
–Nonpayment of Hotel Bill Incl. M64 Games
–Momstercide Again (What's up, Freud?)
–Robin Hooding/Rob-and-Hiding a Chicken
–Other Stuff, Probably

“Baller, we’re famous,” Garindax replied, trying to sound pumped but feeling self-conscious because in most of the pictures his strings looked bassier than he thought they did in real life.

The security guard mud monsters began the redundant processing process.

They sprayed Baron and Garindax with bubblegum-flavored, no-tears decontamination foam; took a few serious mugshot photos and a couple “silly ones”; and outfitted them in Ben Cooper-esque plastic smocks with “Bad Guy 1” and “Bad Guy 2” written across the back.

The duo was then led downstairs into a dungeon where the guards locked the door and ate the key, complete with burp for added effect.

Baron and Garindax looked around at their new home. It was dark and cliché to the max.

Bars and slime-covered stone walls surrounded them on every side. Chained to open treasure chests were spooky, long-bearded skeletons, and chilling in the corner was a toilet pre-filled with a mush mountain of dump.

Baron and Garindax settled in, content with the knowledge that there were definitely worse fates than becoming spooky/rich skeletons with long beards and high-fiber diets.

Suddenly, there was a loud buzz followed by the sound of high heels clacking down the hall.

"*Hello, Fuckface and Fuckface Junior*," a babe voice taunted.

"Oh, shit! Elaine!" Baron yelled pumpedly.

"Am I 'FF' or 'FF Junior'?" Garindax asked concernedly.

"It's *LEILA!*" the babe screamed crabbily.

"Right, right, right. Well, king-fucking-syrup, Leila! You here to bust us out, or what?"

"*What*," she responded, looking more like a mom than ever with her bobbed hair, giant sunglasses, yoga pants, and a latte in each hand. "I'm actually here to torture you."

"Dang."

"You see, after you abandoned me on Sideburn Mountain—"

"*Rescued* you."

"*ABANDONED* me, on Sideburn Mountain, I gave up on the idea of ever getting pumped again. So, I went full adult. I withdrew from all of my necromancy classes and earned a degree in monstorporate communications, with a minor in monsternomics since it was too math-heavy to choose as a major. I had to suck shit and eat rat food through a few unpaid internships, but then I landed my job as Vice Assistant Administrative Torture Process Improvement Specialist at the Monsteropolis Department of Corrections."

"Ah, VAATPIS at the MDOC. Good get," Garindax chimed in because he wanted to feel included.

"How did you do all of that in, like, two days?" Baron asked.

Leila ignored them.

"Now I get paid an ice-cool $23k plus bennies to torture fuckfaces like you: bad guys who live in the pursuit of only what gets *themselves* pumped, even at the expense of society…or girlfriends."

"But why *torture* us? It's not like we have any top-seeks video game tips or funny grandpa stories to share. Just leave us here to chill/die."

"That's *exactly* why I have to torture you. Otherwise, this would be like a vacation. I bet you've already managed to 'get pump' in this jail cell simply because it has skeletons and slime. But even if I put you in a sterile, all-white cell with absolutely no stimulation, you'd probably pretend it's some 'baller ass' futureworld or the dimensional gate room from *Phantasm*."

"It's actually '*pumped-uh.*' But otherwise, wow, dead on," Baron said.

He was shocked by how well Leila knew him even though they had barely hung out. Either he was super one-dimensional, or she was his true soulmate.

"So," she continued, "the only way to punish you for your crimes—including but not limited to leaving me to die/make out with gross rat monsters all across Sideburn Mountain—is to torture you."

"Do your worst," Baron said, feeling somewhat cocky after Leila regarded him as such a resolute pump prophet. "No matter what you do, we'll still find a way to get Pete and Pete."

"Don't start again with that bullshit," Leila snapped. "I realize that you'll never suffer as long as you can use your imagination. So, I had the lab monsters cook up a little something for you."

Leila pulled a syringe from her cleavage. Baron started to pop a boner, but it instantly melted when she spoke her next words:

"An ADHD medicine cocktail! One drop of this, and you'll *NEVER BE PUMPED AGAIN.*"

45

"*NOOOO!*" Baron screamed as Leila walked toward him with the syringe held above her head like a maniac on the loose.

Baron knew he couldn't hurt her because she was still more babe than mom. But he also couldn't think to play any freezing or time-based attacks because of the game show effect.

There was only one way out of the situation, so he took it. He flexed his right bicep, squeezing his fist so hard that his fingernails turned black.

The sight made Leila stop in her tracks and remember her witch/goth roots.

Baron then flexed his left bicep, which most people would expect to be smaller than his right because he was right-handed, but it was for that very reason he worked it out even harder, making it like .25" bigger and 3.82% more vascular.

Leila's pupils turned into voids that sucked in every atom of Baron's rip. Her entire body began to salivate.

Baron brought his arms down across his chest, hitting Leila with a double attack of traps and pecs before closing with the Chong-Li boob dance from *Bloodsport.*

Garindax instinctively started chanting, "Ba-ron! Ba-ron! Ba-ron!" and taking imaginary bets in a beyond-borderline-racist Chinese accent that luckily no one heard.

Leila dropped the syringe, and since she had brought a glass one that she thought looked older/spookier than plastic, it shattered across the cement floor.

Toxic wraith vapors rose from the pool of ADHD medicine and let out a mournful math-equation cry.

"Fuck!" Leila yelled angrily.

Baron flexed his peen muscle.

"*Fuck...*" she whispered sessily.

Her mouth opened and a waterfall of drool poured forth, washing off her red lipstick and revealing the black lipstick she still wore beneath it.

Baron flexed the balls of his feet to launch himself at Leila, and then the balls of his balls to magnetically pull her against him.

The two started making out, hard. Their eyes closed, their tongues wrestled and swapped slime, and a cloud-riding camera monster spun around the room and filmed everything in order to make the scene look more intense/romantic.

"*Yeah, you do it to her, Baron,*" Garindax whispered, trying to be a solid hype man but taking it too far. "You do it to her. You doozy. Watusi. Watusi dat bish. Heh heh. She like it."

Leila opened her eyes and looked over at him.

He was chilling in the corner with a copy of *DeShawn Bitches' Guide to Getting Bitches* and rubbing his strings together while staring up at her with wild spider eyes.

He had pink thing.

Leila's pump insta-drained. She pulled her tongue out of Baron's mouth and pulled his boner out of her crotch.

"I think you both should leave now."

"What the fuck? Why?" Baron demanded. "Because Garindax got pink thing? He can't help it, Leila, he's a guitar."

"I'm just not feeling it anymore."

"But I was going to take you all the way to the Bone Zone."

"Feeling it even less now."

"Lame. Well, you still want to hit Taco Bell or Party City or something? Maybe quest for VHS at ratty shops that reek of cigarettes and where the store owner watches you via CCTV and rubs himself through his sweatpants?"

"Just get out before I decide to torture you again."

"Hey, as if blue balls weren't torture enough!" Baron said in his best Rodney Dangerfield voice.

"*Buh-dum-tsh!*" Garindax rimshotted.

Baron and Garindax cracked up and took turns shouting, "Hey!" and "Hoh!" and "Boy, I tell ya!"

Leila walked across the room and pressed an alarm button on the wall.

"You've got 10 seconds," she said, once again using her mom voice.

"Fart!" Baron yelled. He grabbed Garindax and booked it out of the jail cell.

As sirens blared, the duo tore down corridors and up stairwells, managing to avoid/murder every guard who stood in their way.

Other than a decent miniboss battle against a boar sentinel, though, it wasn't anything they hadn't done a bunch of times already.

"Home free, baby!" Garindax cheered as he and Baron found themselves back in the lobby of the MDOC compound.

But as they busted toward the front door, a giant battle-axe smashed through the wall next to it. A 31' tall, shock blue monster with bat ears, glow-in-the-dark eyes, hooked nose, conical teeth, and hooved pillars of legs exploded into the room with a deafening roar.

A banner reading "WHEN MONSTERS RULED THE MONSTEROPOLIS" fell slowly past his crowned head and draped across his shoulders, giving him a baller cape to complete his already impressive bowtie/suit combo.

Even without a formal introduction, Baron knew from childhood stories and *The Real Ghostbusters* reruns who towered before him:

The Boogeyman.
King of Monsteropolis.
Badass 2DXtreme.
And *final fucking boss monster.*

46

"This is it!" Baron yelled, wielding Garindax and readying his fret-finger callouses.

"Yuh yuh, too crunk!" Garindax yelled back, self-tuning and filling his fangs with every venom known to man/monster.

Baron grimaced and wished Garindax had said pretty much anything else.

The Boogeyman launched the first attack.

He slammed his axe into the ground, sending a shockwave coursing toward Baron.

Baron flipped over it and wailed some swamp metal riffs in midair. The floor beneath Boogey's feet became soft and wet, and the King of Monsteropolis' hooves sank into the dark mire.

Baron landed on solid ground and played harder. He wasn't fucking around since he knew that if he died, the last checkpoint was like 15 obese chef monsters ago.

The ground became swampier, and no matter how much Boogey struggled, he couldn't get out. Still, he laughed.

"Ha! You think a little swampsand will stop *ME?*" he chuckled arrogantly.

"Dude, it already frigg'n has!" Baron snapped back.

King Boogey looked down at his rapidly sinking legs and then cleared his throat.

"You've got me there. But let me tell you, *these hooves were made for walking,*" he sang-said, "*and that's just what they'll do!*"

"Oh my fuck, I hate Monsteropolis so much," Baron sighed.

Boogey stuck his axe into the marshy ground and stirred. The swampsand began to boil, and with a wet sucking sound he burst forth upon a vortex of cyclopean swampranha.

"*And one of these days these hooves are gonna stomp right over you!*" he crooned as he crashed into Baron's chest, catapulting him across the room.

The swampranha vortex followed, and Baron found himself staring down a wave of gnashing teeth, unblinking eyes, and sushi stink.

Even though most of his bones were fucked from the kick (not totally broken, but painful enough to convince a doctor to write some vague bullshit like "hairline dorsal contusions" to get him out of work/gym class for a week), Baron had enough strength to lay out a quick surf melody that materialized into a poisonous fog of crabsquitos, which he hoped would beat swampranha vortices like paper beats rock.

But as soon as he made that tangential connection, his ADHD kicked in.

He thought about how bullshit it used to be when kids would stick out a finger and say "gun" while playing rock, paper, scissors. And then how *extra* bullshit it was when someone countered with "grenade," despite it being the exact same hand gesture as rock. And then Boogey was on top of him and biting his fucking face off.

Garindax knew his buddy was screwed and tattooed if he didn't do something, fast. He pulled himself up by the strings, loaded his omnivenom, and sank his fangs into Boogey's arm. But the monster king's entire body was covered in bitter apple spray since he was training his new pet ferret not to bite, so Garindax recoiled before he could even inject a single drop.

He then tried whipping at Boogey with his razor-wire strings, but Boogey started making weird pleasure grunt sounds, so he stopped that shit as quickly as it started.

In a panic, he pulled up his bud-HUD to discover that Baron's health/pump had already dropped to 25%. Boogey bit him again, and it fell to 16%. Then 7%.

Garindax ran a few calculations slowly because he sucked at multiples of nine, but every one of them pointed to his best friend in the universe being f-bombed. He would be killed with one more bite.

It made Garindax feel sick.

So sick, in fact, that he vommed.

The torrential spray launched up, in, and around King Boogey's face, showering him with the chunks of circus floor popcorn, hotel fries, and goodie (plus a little grossie) that Garindax had eaten during his and Baron's adventure.

"Fucking *GROSS!*" Boogey yelled. He turned his attention to the guitar who was in way over his frets. "What's wrong with you?! And what's wrong with your diet?!"

After spitting a bunch of times and doing some deep breathing, he continued, "I was going to let you watch your friend here die, but now it looks like he'll have the distinct pleasure instead. Or, wait, you'll have the distinct pleasure instead. He'll have the distinct pleasure of watching *you* die, and *you'll* have the distinct pleasure of dying. There, got it."

"No…Garindax…" Baron blood-gurgled as King Boogey released him and grabbed his axe handle with both gnarled hands.

"It's okay, man," Garindax said calmly while closing his spider eyes. "See you in Pumphalla in like two seconds. I'll keep the snowcone machine warmed up for you. Or cooled down. Whichever. Now this dude has me overthinking everything."

Boogey raised his axe above his head, and his eyes went absolutely nuts with rage.

Then pain.

Then confusion.

"*WHAAAT!?*" he shouted, spinning around and swatting the back of his neck.

Baron and Garindax saw it at the same time: the Scarab of Mithyngal.

Garindax had vommed it up along with all the other nonsense, and it was chomping down on King Boogey's maybe-immortal-at-some-point, but-definitely-not-immortal-anymore flesh.

Baron saw his opportunity to attack. But with his health so low, he needed to think of everything he could to get re-pumped:

Halloween theme parks at night.

Dogs sniffing babies and then barking directly in their faces in front of their moms.

The time Garindax took a sip of soda and then disgustedly groaned, "Ugh," and when they looked down at the bottle they saw that someone had scrawled "BAD" on it in Sharpie. But whoever did that still put the soda back in the store's refrigerator and sold it, and whatever was wrong with it Garindax had already consumed.

The time one of his girlfriends took a sip of an energy drink and then disgustedly groaned, "Ugh" and spit out a piece of orange gunk that had been in the can but definitely shouldn't have been.

When he and that same girlfriend were running together at the gym, and after tying her shoe she somehow got a pubic hair in her mouth.

Baron cracked up and instantly reached 100.01% pump. He tried to jump to his feet, but even though his pump was beyond maxed out, his health remained at 7% because health regen didn't exist on Nightmare difficulty. There were only rootbeer health pickups, and they had a crazy low drop rate.

Garindax saw Baron struggling and extended a low E string, more for moral support than anything else.

Baron stuck out a bloody hand and let the string ensnare it. Even though Garindax tried to be gentle, the razor wire sliced into Baron's skin, dropping his health to 1%.

He slammed on his jet boots and hoped that would be enough.

47

Baron rocketed toward Boogey, who had used the ten minutes or so to dislodge the scarab and smash it underhoof. It had done some major damage, though, and the monster king was now flashing red to indicate that he was super low on health, too.

He turned to face Baron and "put an end to this farce" (as he would've said douchely), but instead he caught a flying razor-wire fist straight to the nuts.

The Boogeyman fell to his knees, raised two limp-wristed dinosaur arms, and shimmied back and forth like a moron.

"Finish him!" Garindax yelled.

Baron crouched, kicked, and did a couple punches from a jump distance.

Nothing happened.

"Sweep distance," Garindax corrected.

"Oh, shit, rightrightright," Baron said as he moved closer, or farther, because no one actually knows what the fuck a "sweep distance" is.

Baron crouched, kicked, and punched again.

Suddenly, he was wailing shrill 16-bit notes on a palette-swapped Garindax even though the real one was chilling on the ground next to him.

"*OH FUUUUU—*" Boogey screamed as his eyes popped and his brain blasted out of the open sockets like meat through a grinder. Viscous gore poured forth with the color/intensity of a grape juice box that somebody "accidentally" dropped a backpack on. Finally, his hollow head-o-lantern glowed, flickered, and exploded. Candy rained from the sky, followed by the King of Monsteropolis' crown—which flipped and landed perfectly onto Baron's head.

What remained of The Boogeyman's corpse pissed itself in front of everyone and collapsed into the swampsand.

"*X-Treme Victory! PERFECT!*" the palette-swapped Garindax shouted in a barfy robot voice, despite the fact that it wasn't close to a perfect XTV since Baron had pretty much gotten his ass handed to him.

The Boshi-ass Garindax pixelated into the ether, and Baron walked over and slung the real one over his shoulder.

As they headed to the front door, a familiar babe-voice stopped him.

"*Hey, nice shot.*"

Baron turned and saw Leila standing on a staircase, where she had been chilling for the past 30 minutes just watching and not helping at all.

"You know it," Baron said with a bloody wink. "Thanks for queen-chilling until it was all over, by the way."

"Well, to be honest, I didn't think you were going to win," Leila said unapologetically. "And I only back winners."

"Cool. That's pretty bullshit, but whatever. Now that I'm an 'XTV Perfect' winner, you want to hit up Taco Bell and Party City with us?"

Leila, Baron, and Garindax hopped into her monster sedan with broken air conditioning and headed to the nearest strip mall: Leila talking; Baron blasting/window-drumming along to the first ten seconds of a metal song before getting bored and skipping to the next one; and Garindax sitting in the back-middle seat, so whenever Leila had to look in the rearview mirror to check traffic he would be staring directly into her eyes.

After the trio hit up Taco Bell and Party City (the latter of which most *definitely* had Halloween stuff), Leila came to a stop in the blacklit Belowburbs pumpkin patch where it all began.

There was still no sign of the portal.

"See?" Baron said, pointing. "The portal isn't here anymore. It's gone. It's dead."

"Dead, dead, deadski," Garindax chimed.

"Dead, eh?" Leila replied with a sly smile that was extra red because her lips were still irritated from hot sauce (but not in a defamatory way). "Good thing un-deading stuff is my specialty."

Baron and Garindax didn't know what she was talking about since they had already forgotten that she was a necromancer, but they shrugged and kicked back as Leila stuck her pinkies into the ground and whistled.

The portal exploded open, shooting pink bubbles and milk all over the place.

"*Sweeeeet!*" Garindax screamed. "Time to bust back to Urth, and MF Pizzeria 64!"

Baron was just as pumped, but something held him back—literally.

Leila had him by the shoulder.

"You don't have to go, you know," she closely whispered with hot-sauce breath.

"I made a promise to Little Billy," Baron replied sternly, even though he wasn't sure if he actually did.

"But you can stay here and be king," Leila explained. "You killed The Boogeyman, which means the throne is yours. If you don't accept it, Monsteropolis will be thrown into a new age of war as the remaining blood heirs and total assholes, Prince Kenny and Prince Little Kenny, vie for the crown.

"Please," she pleaded. "Stay and be my king."

"Ha, 'Little Kenny,'" Baron laughed while stepping into the portal. "Being king sounds rad on paper, or I guess in the sky as words, but I know there are a lot of bullshit meetings and stuff that come with it, so fuck' forget it. I also think we have a dog that hasn't been fed in however many days/months we've been here, so he's probably getting hungry."

"Oh, okay," Leila replied dejectedly. "Well, I guess this is 'king see ya' then. Stay pump."

Baron was touched all the way to his butt by her co-opting of his lingo, even if she still didn't have the whole pump/pumped thing down.

"Yo, why don't you come with us?" he asked, extending a hand.

Garindax silently freaked the fuck out.

Leila looked at the ground and shook her head. "You and I could never be together on Urth," she muttered.

Garindax silently chilled the fuck out.

"Why not?" Baron asked. "Just because you're a monster? There are a million witches like you there. You can all hang out in the Occult section at Half-Price Books. It'll be awesome."

"No, it's not that. It's my age. I may be 950 in Monsteropolis years, but in Urth years it's way, way less."

"Like, how less?"

"Like, *you'll go to the Booty House* less."

"Oh, crap. Well, then, yeah. King see ya."

Baron grabbed Garindax and jumped into the portal.

He looked back over his shoulder and saw Leila sadly waving goodbye.

He autist-smiled and waved back, thinking about how he wished he hadn't taken her to the Bone Zone in a Party City dressing room. But what was done was done and, more importantly, geo-contextually legal.

Everything faded to glow-in-the-dark, and then black.

48

As Baron and Garindax began the long jam back to Urth, they reflected upon their time in Monsteropolis while sweet credits music blasted in the background. It was kind of smooth jazzy but upbeat, which helped them feel sentimental about their adventure while not diminishing how action-packed it was.

Baron thought about Leila.

Garindax thought about playing video games and eating room service with his best buddy.

While they reminisced, the names and sprites of all of Monsteropolis' monsters scrolled across the sky. Some were crazy surprising: for instance, the obese chef monsters were actually called "Filet Majors," and there were tiny obese chef monsters called "Filet Minors" that Baron and Garindax never even encountered. They felt a bit gypped, but also kind of pumped because now Monsteropolis had some replay value.

After The Boogeyman and a "Winners Don't Inject Neon Vials of Monster Drugs" message (sponsored by the Director of Monsteropolis' Bureau of Anti-Pump, Harry "Just Harold" Skeener, Esq.) scrolled across the screen, everything faded from black to glow-in-the-dark.

There was a loud *WOOSH!* followed by the sound of a kid's collarbone breaking and a bunch of crying.

Suddenly, Baron and Garindax found themselves chilling in PizzArea 64's ball pit.

Everything looked the same at first, as ball pit technology is relatively static, but the more the two looked around, the more they noticed that this was not the same pizza parlor they had left behind.

All of the arcade machines were now based on crappy mobile phone games.

The only pizza on the menu was an "alkalized, gluten-free, non-GMO, non-allergenic, flavor-free nutritional paste 5D-printed into any shape of your choosing (contingent upon a statistical prediction model demonstrating that a significant majority [$p < .05$] of patrons will not be made uncomfortable by your choice)."

The music sucked.

Worst of all, by the stage and wearing a dusty/decrepit party hat slouched Little Billy. Now he was Big Bill: a retired barber and grandpa whose only remaining thrill in life was an annual "prostrate" checkup.

Baron and Garindax hadn't witnessed horrors half as terrible in a world of nothing but fucking monsters.

Garindax tore through the ball pit and was halfway through the closing portal when Baron pulled him back out.

The portal slammed shut with a soft stink.

"No, Garindax," Baron growled. "Bad Garindax. We just went through all that bullcrap so we could party with Little Billy. And guess what? We're going to party with Little Billy."

Baron leapt out of the ball pit and stretched his fretting fingers.

"Are you the fellas from the cable company?" Big Bill asked with a shaky voice as Baron and Garindax busted up to him.

"NO, LITTLE BILLY," Baron said super loudly and slowly since that's how old people like to be talked to. "IT'S YOUR HOMIES, BARON AND GARINDAX. WE'RE HERE FOR YOUR PARTY."

"Marty? That dog's been dead for decades! She barked in the baby's face. We had no choice, dammit."

"NO, PARTY."

"Jerry? The retarded little Indian boy who works down at Walgreens?"

"NO, PAR-TY."

Big Bill shifted, and Baron heard a diaper crinkle. His pump faltered.

"PAHR-TEE," he enunciated.

"...Spell it."

"P-A-R-T-Y."

"*I know where Alabama is!*" Big Bill snapped. He squinted, then shifted again. There was a much wetter diaper crinkle.

"Garindax?" Baron pleaded.

"*Heeeyyy*, there, Billy Buddy," Garindax tried, using the same tone he uses with cats.

"We came *aaallll* the way back from Monsteropolis just to party with you. Remember us? Cha' boys, Baron and Garindax?"

"Afraid I don't remember much nowadays—um—Zaron and Bindulblax, was it?"

"Baron, actually," Garindax corrected. "But, yeah, I'm Bindulblax."

"Mhm. Greek."

Big Bill stared off into space.

"Like I was saying," he continued after an awkward eternity, "I don't remember too much anymore. Don't even remember why I come here. Just do. Every day. Have for as long as I can remember. Which, like I said, isn't anything to flick your wiener at. Just figure I must be waiting for something, and I'll know it when I see it. But you ain't it. So unless you want to pay my cable bill, you and your little Mormon friend can fart off."

Baron had heard/smelled enough.

He realized the only way to convince Little Billy that it was party time would be to show him, so he kicked through a group of malnourished children who were allergic to everything and leapt onto PizzArea 64's main stage.

The original animatronic mascot band, The Pizzafire Vomsplosion, stood there tinkering on the same instruments as before.

But they no longer played along to "Thriller," "Somebody's Watching Me," or any other songs that easily could've doubled as tracks on a supermarket's Halloween playlist.

Instead, they now played along to minimalistic instrumentation and auto-tuned lyrics telling some generic "baby" how he or she is "perfect/beautiful exactly the way you are, so don't even worry about your personality flaws or the comorbidities of obesity and just be a dumpy, sassy jerk from now till your 25th birthday when you keel over because your heart is tired of trying to pump beef jerky to your limbs."

To reach Big Bill, Baron would have to drown out the music.

He would have to drown it.

He would have to bite gently on its fingernails and make little bird noises to lure it into a false sense of security before going crazy and biting super hard until the nails turn purple and split down the middle and shoot blood/cuticles all over the place.

It was time to fucking party.

Baron bypassed all power chords and began shredding a series of insane black metal solos on Garindax, who held a spider shriek so deep that the reverberations produced double-bass drum sounds.

It was ultimately cacophonic yet ultimately *pumped.* At that precise moment, ADHD metal was born.

The Pizzafire Vomsplosion tried to keep up, but it was impossible. Because they believed there to be no point in pursuing music/life if they couldn't be the best (an insecurity instilled in them by their literal helicopter parents), they started mercy killing each other.

The drummer, a large walrus robot, grabbed his drumsticks and stabbed them into the neck of the generic Italian plumber bassist. With one quick twist, the plumber's eyes rolled into the back of his head and his lips curled into a smile for the first time since before "the water backpack incident" of 2002.

The walrus returned the smile as his chest exploded, sending bolts and sparks flying into the crowd of horrified children. A banjo neck stuck through his heart-gears and brought them to a screeching halt. Behind the gears and through the walrus' open back, a coonhound banjoist wept violently.

"Fucking do it already!" he begged. The beautiful shark vocalist, with saltwater tears streaming down her face, acquiesced. She snapped her jaw around the coonhound's waist. His pupils widened, and with another chomp, he was cut into two rough halves.

Oil and coolant poured across the stage, sending the shark belly-sliding into the crowd.

There were no band members left. To end her own misery, she would have to resort to suicide-by-technician and violate Law 1.

She bit the nearest bystander.

Big Bill.

"*You son of a bitch!*" he yelled as her serrated teeth cut through his liver-spotted arm like unrefrigerated olive loaf.

Old people tend to spit whenever they yell/chew/breathe/fight robots, and Big Bill was no exception. A stream of butterscotch saliva launched from his mouth down the shark's throat and into her bowel CPUs, causing a chain reaction that short-circuited everything but her robot shark boobs, which began to bounce like fucking crazy.

Every gerbil-haired adolescent (dudes, chicks, nonbinaries, dragonkin, etc. because this was a more modern time) immediately busted out their cell phones and filmed the scene for "later use" (because despite it being a more modern time, some things hadn't changed).

Baron stopped playing Garindax and rushed to Big Bill's side, kicking aside the shark robot who was quickly dragged off to the ball pit by the ratty teens.

"Little Billy!" Baron screamed. "Are you okay?"

"Heh, boy oh boy, that was one hell of a party," Big Bill laughed.

"Party…

"Shit, it's really you…isn't it? Baron…and Garindax. I remember now. The fog is starting to clear, boys. I…remember.

"Oh…I've waited so long…

"And now…we finally…partied…

"And…I…finally…got…pumped…

"I'm…pumped…dudes…

"I'm…pumped…

"I'm…going…nuts…"

Big Bill sputtered, coughed up a bit of blood/applesauce, and crashed to the floor.

Baron knelt and checked Big Bill's pulse.

"I'm afraid he's fried eggs," he exhaled sadly.

"What does that mean again?" Garindax asked.

"He's dead, dude."

"Dang…"

"Yep…"

"Well, good thing we both have a girlfriend whose specialty is un-deading stuff!"

"Too soon, man," Baron sighed.

He straightened Little Billy's party hat and placed gold tokens over his eyes. He then plucked one of the hairs from Little Billy's head and ate it so they'd always be a part of each other. Garindax understood the sentiment, but it still made him feel funny.

Baron sheathed Garindax and trudged out of PizzArea 64's Ballerific Birthday Blastorium.

He was on a pump rollercoaster so nuts, it only could've existed in Tokyo.

On the one hand, he was bummed that Little Billy had become Big Bill and then Dead Bill. On the other hand, he understood that there were worse fates than frying eggs in the jaws of a robot shark vocalist whose boobs were going absolutely fucking ballistic.

As Baron's pumpcoaster finally began to achieve equilibrium, a familiar voice called out to him and almost sent it flying off the tracks.

49

"Hello, babies!" the nasally voice rasped.

It was the nerd ticket station attendant.

He, like Big Bill, was now an old dude. Unlike Big Bill (and as predicted), he was a *non*-grandpa who had never dunked a basketball or made out with a babe or anything. So, he never had kids/grandkids, which is how that shit works.

Baron and Garindax busted straight past him without looking over and bailed out of PizzArea 64. They were done with bullshit for the day.

"Yeah, that's right," the ancient nerd chuckled insecurely. "You better run, little boys."

He was secretly devastated, though, for he also had been anxiously awaiting the duo's return. The moment he busted someone as badass as Baron over the difference between *ESM 4* and *ESM 5* had been the highlight of his entire life, and ever since then he had hoped to recapture the high of that day.

But Baron hadn't even looked over at him, and now he was gone.

And now the nerd had nothing left to live for.

He clutched his chest and collapsed to the threadbare neon carpet.

As he lay dying, he realized that he would never be rich/famous, nor would he ever suck on a pair of babe-nips. He had always imagined that he would have all of those things. All it would've taken was one comic he never drew, one tabletop game he never designed, or one "Let's Play" video he never filmed to get crowdfunded for the millions of dollars he knew his ideas were worth.

But he hadn't created anything other than a lot of trash and a lot of dump.

He imagined the mountains of both that were his legacy and immediately vommed up a slurry of half-digested PizzaQuesaDipper Bites, their respective habanero ghost pepper ranch sauce, and a gallon of what he dubbed "Call of Dewtea" (a mixture of store-brand Dew and sweet tea).

He reached up to the passing moms and dads, whom he still viewed as "grownups" even though they were all 30-40 years younger, but no one helped him because he was an ugly old man and an absolute stranger.

They weren't wrong. After his mom and dad died in a car accident, he became a stranger to the entire world.

He thought about his parents often.

He thought about how much they had loved him, and how they had given him the last hug he ever felt—or would feel.

He thought about how he played *ESM 16* through their funeral because it didn't seem real, or so it wouldn't. He thought about how ever since their funeral, he dreamed of them almost every night.

In his dreams, he and his parents were vibrant and happy in his childhood home: where nothing had changed. But then he would awaken in his dark studio apartment and remember that *everything* had changed. Someone else was living in that house, and his parents weren't living at all.

Before he could cry, he would reach for his phone and *Escape from Sideburn Mountain.*

Escape from everything.

Tears welled in his eyes. But his phone was on the ticket redemption counter, and he was on the floor.

He cried openly.

The world continued walking by.

He wondered if there would be an afterlife, where maybe he could see his parents again, where maybe he could do things differently.

Just, do things.

He felt a twinge of hope, but it was quickly ripped away by the realization that, if there were an afterlife, he hadn't done anything to deserve a good one—or a bad one.

He vomited again, but this time it caught in his throat. He tried coughing, but nothing came up.

His esophagus burned.

He couldn't breathe.

He began to count backward, a technique that always calmed him down whenever he couldn't play *ESM* because it was updating.

It didn't help.

Panic set in.

He could feel his heartbeat in his eyes.

He thought of a continue screen.

He began to count faster.

"Fuck yeah, we're finally home!" Baron yelled as he and Garindax jet-boot descended to their ratty apartment complex.

Bricks were cracked and missing; the roof was blanketed in beer bottles and dead birds; and the pool, despite its "Sorry Close" sign, was filled with chubby kids wearing t-shirts and splashing waterlogged bees/wasps at each other to see who would get stung first.

Everything was almost exactly the way Baron and Garindax remembered it. The only thing off, both figuratively and literally, was their front door.

50

The duo cautiously but pissed-pumpedly busted into their living room/dining room/kitchen (it was a pretty shitty apartment).

"Oh, fucknockers!" Garindax shouted.

"What?! What'd you see?!" Baron replied.

"Nothing. I just remembered that we forgot to give LB the pocketknife."

Before Baron could respond, a cupboard door exploded opened and an almost perfectly spherical child spilled onto the laminate floor.

He grunted, stood up, brushed cookie crumbs off his tattered cloak, and attempted to wipe the snowcone syrup off his face but instead got a bunch of cookie crumbs stuck to it. He then waddled silently (except for some asthmatic wheezing) toward Baron, who wielded Garindax and fingered a barre chord in anticipation.

The kid stopped short and pulled a crumpled piece of notebook paper from his cloak. He grunted again, and then struggle-read in his best Rodney Dangerfield voice, "Yo, Dark Pops! Hey! How the hell are ya? Let's see, what else, what else…Oh, yeah! You maybe thought you had pumped and adventure, but Mom says you should prolly see something. To see them to. To see them, too."

The kid definitely had ADHD, but Baron wasn't about to accept some shit that required time and money without being a hundo percent sure it was his. He walked over to the kid and snagged the note.

The scent of hot sauce and witch boobs danced off the paper and into his nostrils.

Baron had no idea what the kid thought he was reading, as the letter contained a message that was far more articulate/intense:

Babyron (Baby Baron) is yours now because he's annoying as fuck and I can't deal.

<3—Leila
Mommy Blogger and Amateur Nutritionist
Actually, Expert Nutritionist

Baron slapped five hard with his kid, whom he insta-renamed Ultra Slaughterhouse because there was zero fucking chance he was going to raise a kid with "Baby" in his name.

Baron, Garindax, and Ultra Slaughterhouse didn't know what lay ahead of them: they might go on a quest back to Monsteropolis to find Leila and ask for some fun money, they may collect half-full cans of soda/beer from construction sites and then pour the contents over crushed ice and sell them as "homemade snowcones" from a stand outside a minor league baseball stadium, or they might just kick back and watch cartoons on VHS until their buttholes hurt.

No matter which adventure they chose, it was destined to be *PUMPED AS FUCK.*

Codes

2235-EFAF	Infinite pump
A23F-7464	Infinite health
A26A-87A7	Infinite lives*
7D33-8FDF	Infinite jet boots
BF2T-AABJ	Infinite venom
AZ2T-AAA6	Start at 1% health**
J32T-AAB6	Start with max snowcones
GP0A-AAB2	Play as palette-swapped Garindax
NS4T-AAFN	Accidentally walk in on your friend's mom when she's getting out of the shower***
THNX-MANG	Thanks for reading!

NOTES

*: Game will freeze if you are bitten by the Scarab of Mithyngal.

**: Whoever used codes like this is now either crazy rich or crazy dead.

***: Not an accident.

64 with Expansion Pack (Alternate Ending)

The camera zooms over a bunch of fields and finally stops on a nest of Boogeyman eggs in a barn somewhere.

"What the FUCK is this monstrosity?" Baron yelled.

Dweem tracked the voice and waddle-ran over. "Pops! What's wrong?"

"There's a fucking *Eiffel Tower* in the middle of the park? How BABY ASS! Plus, how is that even Christmassy?"

Dweem sighed in relief.

"I wonder if it's too late to get a refund," Baron said as he headed back toward the entrance.

"Dude, just ignore it," Garindax replied. "And check out all the cool shit that's *around* it."

Baron scoped out the sights: directly in front of him, an ornate fountain shot red and green ice water all over the place. On both sides of the tower, sidewalks were lined with candy canes, incandescent Christmas lights, bigass gumdrops, and biggerass gingerbread houses.

"Oh, damn, true," Baron gasped. "Talk about scraping the goodie off."

"Now you got it," Garindax responded.

Dweem had no idea what they were talking about since Scrape the Goodie Off closed shortly after he was born in Monsteropolis, and the one time his dad tried to tell him about his and Garindax's adventures there, Dweem zoned out around the Mrs. Bones part.

"Well, let's not fuck around, shall we?" Baron announced. "We all came here for one reason, so let's get to it. That sign over there says Santa is at 'Ye Olde Nog Lodge.' Looks like it's straight ahead, past all of the rollercoasters, arcades, and pizza bounce houses."

Dweem began to sweat more than usual. "We get to do some of that stuff first, though, right? Like, at least the pizza bounce house? I don't even know what that is, but somehow it's all I've ever wanted in life."

"No frigg'n way. I'm a dad, so we gotta stay on schedule. Look, I have a list and everything." He pulled out a crumpled-up sheet of legal paper comprising a list of chores related to yards, garages, hardware stores that reeked of pesticide, and dry cleaners that also reeked of pesticide.

"See?" he said proudly. "Them's the bricks, kid. That's a saying, right? Them's the road? I dunno. A fucking chore list."

"Me, too," Garindax said as he produced a tiny list from his output jack.

Dweem strained his eyes to read what was written in spider-scrawl: *Chill, mostly, but also clean NBs.*

"What are NBs?" Dweem asked.

"New Balances," Baron and Garindax replied in unimpressed unison. "Geez, it's like you're not even a dad."

The trio beelined straight to Ye Olde Nog Lodge: a large, wooden banquet hall that looked like a toy cabin had it starred in the movie *Honey, I Blew Up the Christmas*; its porn parody, *Honey, I Blew Up the Christmas All Over Your Face*; or its porn parody sequel, *Honey, I Blew Up the Christmas All Over Your Face 2: Honey, I Blew the Christmas.*

"Wow!" Dweem exclaimed as he spun around and soaked in every holly-jolly sight, sound, and smell.

To his right was a tiny fudgery, where a cheery Mrs. Claus pumped out log after log of the good stuff. To his left loomed aisles of t-shirts featuring the holographic or lenticular visages of Kristmas Kingdom's mascots, like Dweasel the Reindeer and Boosnoos the Snowdogclown.

In the far corner stood a makeshift shop that sold nothing but pristine, brand-new Sega Saturn games for crazy cheap. In the other corner, an animatronic/anthropomorphic corncob with a straw hat and a piece of straw hanging from his mouth churned butter. It looked over at Dweem and winked.

"Oooh," Dweem moaned as he entered sensory/pump overload. He spun around harder and squeezed his bosoms together in pure, Christmas glee. "What to do *fiiiirst?*"

"None of this bullshit," Baron growled. "It's Santa time, son. Do you need to see the chore lists again?"

Dweem's pump plummeted as Baron grabbed his hand and pulled him to the center of the lodge, where Santa king-chilled on a silver throne, which throne-chilled on a golden dais.

"Yo, Santa," Baron began sternly. "We got a shit-ton of wishes and a rabbit-poop of time."

"Ho ho ho!" Santa laughed. "Isn't that a delightful little phrase. A 'rabbit-doodie of time!'"

"Poop," Baron corrected.

"Shit," Garindax added.

"Don't you get it, Dad?" Dweem said with a nudge. "He's a Santa. Santas don't curse. They're like Mormons."

"Oh damn," Baron replied.

"Dang," Dweem corrected.

"Darn," Santa hundo corrected.

"So, y'all also don't drink caffeine, and you have a bunch of wives and stuff?" Garindax asked.

"We're not allowed to drink coffee or tea, but for some reason Coke is okay—even Monster. And the wife stuff is just Fundamentalist Santas. That's a whole different thing."

"Well, I don't agree with it, but I respect it," Baron brown-nosed. "Now about our wishes."

"I'm afraid you'll have to wait in line, young men," Santa said kindly. "But I can't wait to hear them. I bet they're *terrific* wishes."

Baron turned around into a sea of crabby mom and bummed baby faces.

"Oh damn, sorry," Baron said because he knew he had to stay halfway decent until he got his wish. "I mean, darn."

He, Garindax, and Dweem busted to the back of the line and waited behind a group of goth teens who claimed to be taking the picture with Santa ironically. They kept calling him "Satan Claws"; threw up the horns because they thought it was hilarious; and when they finally got to Santa, the one girl in the group tried to sit on his lap so she could look cool/sessy in the picture, but when he was like "Nah, we don't do that here," she got offended and frowned more than usual and afterward told everyone outside that Santa was a "filthy pervert" even though he didn't do *anything*.

After 900 years, it was the trio's turn to approach the silver-and-gold throne.

"That was quick, boys," Santa said with a smile.

"We're not wasting any time. We got STDs."

Santa's smile quickly dropped.

"Oh, I see. Well, then, I suppose you'll be wishing for penicillin in your stockings."

"Nah, fu—er, fart that. We don't need drugs. Prolly just snag a couple energy drinks and knock it out."

"Energy drinks. For STDs?"

"Yeah, man. Nothing like a, um, shoot-ton of caffeine when you got stuff to do."

"Ah, ho ho ho!" Santa laughed. "Stuff to do! How delightful. But why is 'stuff to do' STDs, plural?"

"Because there's more than one stuff to do."

"Then why not 'stuffs to do'?"

"SsTD?" *S's* to do?" Baron mulled. "Nah, man. We're not trying to 'do' any s's. That goth chick was right about you. You're a little freaky-deaky."

"Hmm. What's your wish?" Santa said, beginning to lose his saintly patience.

"I wish for—"

"Mom and Dad to be friends again!" Dweem shouted as he pushed past Baron.

"Well, isn't that a beautiful wish!" Santa roared in delight.

"Oh, somebody is about to get the fart—nah, the *fuck*—grounded," Baron growled.

"Now, now," Santa chided. "This young man is so passionate about reconciling his parents that he couldn't wait a second longer, and I think that's just fine. Tell me, lad, who's your daddy, and why did he and your mommy break up?"

"He's—" Dweem started. This time, Baron cut him off.

"What do you mean, 'Who's your daddy?' I'm standing right here. You should know that."

"Ah, but, um, of course!" The Santa laughed. "Just an old Santa trick."

He winked, but no sprinkle nor sparkle nor candy cane dust came out of his eye pocket: only a tiny, not-even-Christmas-green eye booger.

"Yeah frigg'n right!" Baron shouted as he put the pieces together. "Tell me, what's this dude's name?"

He spun around to reveal Garindax on his back. The guitar/spider monster winked all eight eyes, and sparkles went everywhere.

"What the FUCK is that?!" Santa screamed so loudly that his beard flew off and onto Dweem's chubby hamster cheeks.

"I knew it!" Baron declared. "You're not the real Santa!"

"No," Dweem said as he straightened his new fake beard. "I am."

"You're fucking grounded is what you are," Baron snapped as he snatched the beard off Dweem. He threw it back at the was-a-Santa, now-just-a-stranger.

"Your beard's fake, and so are you! And look at those acne scars. Fucking gross!"

"You're right," the impostor said sadly. "I'm not Santa. My real name is Buttbutt. And I got pimples when I was a kid because I would eat straight butter, or sometimes butter with little dinosaur fruit snacks jammed into it so it looked like they were stuck in a tar pit."

"Santa...you're not real?" Dweem stammered.

"Buttbutt," Garindax corrected excitedly.

"You're just some fat, pockmarked guy named Buttbutt..." Dweem trailed off.

"I'm sorry," Buttbutt apologized.

"So, there really is no Santa. And I'll never get my one, true Christmas wish."

Baron cringed at his kid saying "one, true Christmas wish." *It's one thing to hit up a magical dude and tell him what you want so you get it*, he thought, *but Dweem is making it too weird/baby, plus he's way too old for this shit.*

"Yeah, Buttbutt sucks," he said. "Let's get out of here. Well, Dweem, *you* get out of here. Your uncle and I are gonna 'hang around' for a bit."

Baron and Garindax chuckled as the latter unwound two of his strings and made them dance around like little nooses.

"Hey, make it three," Buttbutt said with a smile.

"Hell no," Baron snapped. "You made my kid realize there's no such thing as Santa/magic, so you're not getting shit except maybe a couple swift kicks to the ping-pong."

"Yeah, Buttbutt," Garindax chimed in because he was really enjoying the name.

"Wait a present-picking-second," the impostor said while covering his crotch. "Now, I never said there was *no such thing* as the real Santa."

"I'm listening," Baron said.

Dweem turned his head hopefully, his chubby little meatball eyes growing in wonderment.

Fake Santa leaned in closely and whispered, "The real Santa is right here. In this park."

"But you just said that you *weren't* Santa," Dweem said exasperatedly.

"And you have doodoo bref," Garindax added.

Baron cracked up. "We should start calling him Doodoo instead of Buttbutt. Or Buttbref. Doodoobref. Doodoo Buttbref Island Man."

"Shut the fuck up for half a second, you idiots," Buttbutt snarled.

None of the trio was surprised Buttbutt cursed because they knew that since he wasn't actually Santa, he no longer had to be Mormon-nice. A bunch of kids started crying, though, and moms began letting the Yelp reviews *fly*.

"Well, there goes my job," Buttbutt sighed. "And Christmas for my kids. Thanks a lot."

He rose from his Santa throne and headed to the door.

"Wait!" Baron yelled as he followed. "You still have to tell us about the real Santa."

"I don't have to do shit for you now that you got me fired. Get fucked. Badbye."

"Pwease, Santa man," Dweem called from behind them. Baron and Buttbutt turned to find Dweem sitting in Santa's throne, trying to look like a sad puppy with developmental issues. But since he was just a dumpy fat kid or possibly a dumpy fat adult with a greasy bowl cut and clothes that smelled like porta-potty-aged cheese, it looked pathetic in a way that he wasn't going for at all.

Baron frowned and shook his head in fatherly disappointment, and Buttbutt shook his head in fake-Santaly disappointment.

"Man, y'all are annoying," he muttered. "I mean you're just *genuinely* unlikeable people."

"And guitar/spider monster," Garindax added.

"Oh yeah, and guitar/spider monster. How could I ever forget something so *cool?*" the Santa impostor said sarcastically.

He was really starting to act like a dick, but Baron let it slide in order to hear about the top seeks.

Luckily, his patience paid off.

"Look," Buttbutt began, "I'll tell you the secret a) if you leave me alone and b) because you'll probably get killed on your quest."

"Deal," Baron agreed.

"This park…it changes at night. Just wait till 12:25 CM, and you'll see."

"CM?"

"*Christmas Magic* time. Not *Child Molester* time, or *Chinese Moomoo* time, or anything else stupid or offensive. So, don't even start."

"Whoa, project much?" Baron replied indignantly, even though he was trying hard not to crack up at Chinese Moomoo time.

"Sorry, I'm just tired. Y'all are tiring. Stay here till 12:25 CM. That's when their haunted houses open. That's when they all come out."

Baron became insta-intrigued. "Whoa, who?"

"The 13 Creeps. The 13 Creeps of Christmas. Spooky Basement Volume 2: The 13 Creeps of Christmas."

Made in the USA
Middletown, DE
12 August 2019